TYPICALLY JENNINGS!

More Jennings books
to watch out for:

1. JENNINGS GOES TO SCHOOL
2. THANKS TO JENNINGS
3. ESPECIALLY JENNINGS
4. JENNINGS IN PARTICULAR
5. SPEAKING OF JENNINGS
6. TRUST JENNINGS
8. THE JENNINGS REPORT
9. JENNINGS OF COURSE
10. ACCORDING TO JENNINGS

and the brand-new Jennings book
JENNINGS AGAIN!

Author's note

Each of the Jennings books is a
story complete in itself. Apart
from the first title, JENNINGS
GOES TO SCHOOL, the books
can be read in any order, and for
this reason I have chosen some of
the later titles for early
publication in this edition.

Anthony Buckeridge

TYPICALLY
JENNINGS!

Anthony Buckeridge

MACMILLAN CHILDREN'S BOOKS

For
Sarah Jane
and
Roger Ardley

First published 1971 by William Collins & Sons Co Ltd
Paperback edition, with illustrations by Rodney Sutton, published
1990 by PAN MACMILLAN CHILDREN'S BOOKS
A division of Pan Macmillan Publishers Limited
London and Basingstoke
Associated companies throughout the world

Reprinted 1991, 1992

ISBN 0-333-49689-2

A CIP catalogue record for this book is
available from the British Library

Printed in England by Clays Ltd, St Ives plc

CONTENTS

Chapter	Page
1 The Rickety Racket	1
2 The Umpire's Decision	13
3 Sale Price	21
4 The Hide-out	34
5 Quiet Commentary	48
6 Thunder in the Air	61
7 The Bogus Bug-Hunters	73
8 Doubtful Security	87
9 Blow-up	100
10 Prehistoric Joke	114
11 Restricted Access	130
12 Full Circle	141

LIST OF
ILLUSTRATIONS

"I'm terribly sorry but something terrible's
happened," said Darbishire.   10

"Wow! Perhaps it's a smugglers' cave,"
said Darbishire.   43

"Why on earth don't you look where you're
going, you clumsy little boy?" exclaimed
the headmaster.   74

The cooking-stove had blown itself to
smithereens.   111

Venables and Temple shot out through the
cave mouth.   121

Chapter 1

The Rickety Racket

Darbishire's tennis racket looked like an Eskimo's snow-shoe after Jennings had run over it with the garden roller.

Admittedly, it was only an old racket with a lop-sided frame and had never been much use in the first place. Furthermore, the accident was pure mischance: it was not the sort of thing that Jennings would have planned on purpose.

But these excuses were beside the point, the victim maintained. The racket belonged to him – C.E.J. Darbishire, aged eleven, of Linbury Court School – and he had every right to feel incensed at this outrageous treatment of his personal property.

"Ruined it – that's what you've done," he stormed, waving the buckled object in the air. "It's no good for anything now." Angrily, he took a swipe at a passing mosquito, missing it by inches. "There you are, you see! That proves it. It isn't even any use as a fly-swatter now – thanks to you."

"Sorry, Darbi, I didn't mean to," Jennings said humbly. "I was just going to flatten out that bump near the net and suddenly the roller got away from me and – well, what happened next—"

"You don't have to tell me," Darbishire broke in. "I *saw* what happened next."

He didn't need Jennings to remind him! . . . He had just put his racket down on the grass and was winding up the net, when out of the corner of his eye he had glimpsed his companion trundling the roller along the crest of the bank just behind the junior court.

Darbishire had paid little attention to his friend's antics: Jennings was always charging around interfering with things that didn't concern him. If he really wanted to be helpful, he could flipping well come and lend a hand in winding up the net instead of—

Suddenly, there had been a shout of alarm from the top of the bank, and the next moment the roller was careering down the slope with Jennings tugging at the handle trying to check its momentum. Faster and faster it clanged and rattled down the incline, dragging the boy behind it, his body straining backwards like a reluctant water-skier and his feet back-pedalling wildly to save himself from falling.

At the bottom of the bank Jennings lost his hold and the roller sped on towards the tennis court, heading straight for the startled figure by the net-post. Darbishire leapt like a mountain goat: the roller rumbled past him, narrowly missing the post and slowing to a stop some twenty yards farther on.

It was then that Darbishire had let out his first wail of protest . . . In the swathe of turf flattened by the passage of the roller, his racket, bent, buckled and battered, lay pressed into the grass . . . He'd seen it happen! He didn't need Jennings to fill in the details . . .

"You're a dangerous maniac, Jen! You're not fit to be in charge of a supermarket trolley – let alone a great jumbo-jet of a garden roller," Darbishire protested. "Besides, you're not allowed to touch the thing without permission. Old Wilkie would have blown his top if he'd seen you."

"I've said I'm sorry. And anyway, I was doing it for you really," the culprit defended himself. "You know how your famous serves always shoot off sideways when they hit that bump."

"Doing it for me!" Darbishire snorted with derision. "You bulldoze my racket into the ground and try to murder me into the bargain, and then turn round and say you were doing it for my sake."

"I *didn't* try to murder you!"

"That's what you say! I know better. You tried, but you didn't succeed." Darbishire was determined to make the most of his grievance. By ignoring the facts and adding a few touches from his imagination, he was able to portray the accident as a diabolical plot. "I was too quick for you: I frustrated your crafty plan. I saw the missile hurtling towards me, and in the nick of time I jumped."

"Sounds quite exciting when you put it like that," Jennings said approvingly. "Let's have another go and see if I can polish you off properly this time."

There was a casual, easy-going relationship between the two boys that could swing from friendship to hostility and back again in the course of a few moments: for the friendship was deep-rooted, and the hostility no more than the short-lived exasperation of two eleven-year-olds sharing the day-to-day frustrations of school rules and school routine.

Despite their close friendship, the boys were unlike each other in appearance and temperament. Jennings, tall for his years, was impulsive and lively with a wide-awake look in his eyes. Darbishire was cautious by nature and deliberate in speech. In moments of crisis it was Jennings who made the decisions and Darbishire who did what he was told. It was Jennings who acted first and thought afterwards, and Darbishire who could never quite make up his mind. In theory, they may have seemed an ill-assorted pair; in practice, they were well-suited to help each other to cope with the exploits and misadventures of boarding-school life.

Darbishire tossed the broken racket over his shoulder and said, "So much for my chances of winning the junior tournament this term. It's really hard luck, you know, when a bloke's whole future on the courts is cut short just because some other bloke starts fooling around with dangerous rollers."

"Stop being so sorry for yourself," Jennings said severely. "It wasn't you that got hurt – it was just your tatty old fly-swatter of a racket. You must admit it wasn't any good. It's been falling to bits for ages."

"I dare say, but at least it was something to play with," Darbishire argued. "Now, I haven't got an excuse to use the court any more."

This was the real point of his protest. Though practically useless as a sporting implement, the racket had been his passport to the world of tennis, enabling him to skip around the junior court after prep on fine summer evenings, lobbing balls hopefully towards the sagging net. But now he had lost his claim: boys who had rackets (of an acceptable shape) could use the court; boys who hadn't, couldn't.

Jennings retrieved the racket from the tufty grass

beyond the sideline and examined it. "I'll try and mend it for you," he offered.

"Mend it! *You*!" Darbishire raised despairing eyes towards the setting sun. "I can just imagine what it would be like by the time you'd finished thumping it about with your great maulers. It's got to look like a tennis racket – not a shrimping net."

"All right then, I'll tell you what I'll do. As it was my fault, I'll buy you a new one."

"Honestly?" Darbishires's eyes sparkled. This was more than he'd hoped for!

"A new second-hand one," Jennings amended hastily. "It'd be a waste of money buying a new one for your sort of tennis. Everyone knows you play like a pigeon-toed newt in dark glasses."

Darbishire ignored the insult and counted his blessings. A second-hand racket would be just the thing: he didn't really need a good one. It was true what they said about his tennis. If he was honest with himself, he was bound to admit that he *did* play rather like a pigeon-toed newt.

Together they towed the roller back to its accustomed place. They had to make a detour to avoid dragging it up the bank – a task which would have been beyond their strength. So they followed the path skirting the senior courts, where the surface was smoother and the grass was greener than on the court used by the younger boys.

Away to their right was the cricket field and beyond that the playground and the school buildings. To their left, rough meadow grass sloped down to the little wood and the marshy pond at the far end of the school grounds.

They had just replaced the roller when Venables, Temple and Atkinson, brandishing their rackets like tomahawks, came charging across the cricket field heading for the junior court.

Darbishire snorted in exasperation. "Fat lot of good it was getting down here early, if Venables' lot are going to bag the court after all."

The rule on this point was clear. At the end of prep the first juniors to reach the court could claim possession; and on this particular June evening Jennings and Darbishire had slipped out of the building well ahead of their friends and would, by this time, have been halfway through their set if it had not been for the accident with the roller. Now they would have to forgo their claim, and the rival contenders could look forward to enjoying forty minutes of unskilful play before the dormitory bell.

Venables, a gangling, untidy boy of twelve, reached the court first and began to wind up the net. Close behind him came the stocky, square-rigged Temple and the fair-haired, excitable Atkinson.

Temple glanced up at the bank and called, "Hey, Darbi, want to make up a foursome?"

Darbishire pulled a face. "I can't. Jennings has gone and bust my racket for me."

"How about you then, Jennings?"

"Yes, all right. I'll play."

Jennings was at the bottom of the bank when Darbishire's cry of protest shattered the peace of the summer evening.

"Hey, that's not fair! You can't ask him instead of me."

"Why not?" Temple could see nothing wrong with the arrangement. "If you've got nothing to play with, that's

6

your bad luck, isn't it!" He stood by the net-post, waving his racket like a semaphore flag. "Come on, Jennings, toss for partners, shall we?"

Jennings hesitated, and then swung round to his friend. "Go on then, Darbi. You can play instead of me. I'll lend you my racket."

"Coo, really great of you." All cares forgotten, Darbishire slithered down the slope and rushed off to retrieve Jennings' racket which was lying on the grass. Then, touched by his friend's self-sacrifice, he shouted, "Hey, Jen, I didn't *really* think you were trying to murder me. I just said that to make you feel guilty."

"*I'll* murder you if you don't stop talking rubbish," Venables threatened. He had wound up the net and was anxious to start the game. "I'll tell you what – we'll have a famous outer-space tournament: Temple and me, the greatest players on Mars, challenge Atki and Darbi, the world-famous tennis stars of the moon."

"You mean moon-famous – not world-famous," Atkinson argued. "How can you have stars on the moon? I doubt if they could even play tennis up there, with those bumpy old craters all over the surface."

Leaving the Martians and the moon-dwellers to settle their interplanetary arguments, Jennings wandered back across the games field, practising service shots with his friend's useless racket. Little clouds of mosquitoes scattered as he smote the air, only to close in again and swarm round his perspiring forehead as he stood poised for his next stroke.

The games field was dotted with short-sleeved figures enjoying the last hour of free time before the dormitory bell . . . Mr Carter, the senior master, and his colleague Mr Wilkins were bowling at the 1st XI cricket nets.

Behind the nets, Rumbelow was kneeling down practising the recorder, his music spread out on the grass. Over by the long-jump pit Binns and Blotwell, the youngest boys in the school, were playing golf with ping-pong balls and walking-sticks. Martin-Jones was trying to do handstands against the wall of the scoring box. Nuttall and Johnson were gathering leaves for their caterpillars from the hedge by the headmaster's garden. It was, in short, a scene of carefree activity such as could have been observed on almost any fine evening during the summer term.

Once past the games field Jennings crossed the playground, heading for the side entrance to the main school block. Just outside the door he found Bromwich, a fellow third-former, sitting on the bottom step rocking with silent laughter.

"What's the joke?" he asked.

Bromwich controlled his mirth with an effort. "Terribly funny, really! There was this bloke with a dog, you see, and he said to his friend, 'My dog's got no nose,' and the other bloke said, 'Got no nose, how does he smell?' and the first bloke said, 'He smells terrible'."

"That's as stale as a school bun," Jennings said scathingly. "I heard that joke a hundred years ago."

"Well, I didn't know it before. I've just heard it on the radio."

"Radio!" For a moment Jennings was puzzled. Then he noticed the tiny earphone that Bromwich was wearing and saw the plastic-covered lead disappearing into the breast pocket of his blazer. "Oh, I see! I didn't know you'd got a radio."

"Had it last week for my birthday," Bromwich

replied proudly, producing the instrument for Jennings' inspection.

It was the smallest radio set that Jennings had ever seen – scarcely bigger than a matchbox and certainly smaller than his grandmother's hearing-aid. There was no loudspeaker, so the sound was audible only to the listener with the earphone. He took the set from Bromwich and listened. Though the range was limited, the tone was loud and clear. "Really great," he approved.

"I wanted a small one for listening under the bed-clothes," Bromwich explained. "Matron won't be able to see it in my pyjama pocket."

Jennings was struck with further possibilities. "You could use it in class, if you wanted to."

Bromwich looked doubtful. "They might see the wire. I don't want to get it confiscated."

He was immensely proud of his latest possession and spent some time in demonstrating its merits. He was still trying unsuccessfully to tune in to a continental station when Mr Carter's whistle sounded the end of evening break.

Jennings was on the way up to his dormitory a few minutes later when Darbishire caught him up on the first landing. From the worried look on his face it was clear that he had a confession to make.

"Hey, Jen, I'm terribly sorry but something terrible's happened," he began. "I've put my foot through your tennis racket."

The vaguest hint of a suspicion flashed through Jennings' mind. "On purpose, you mean? Just to get your own back?"

Darbishire was shocked by the suggestion. "Oh, fish-hooks, no! Honestly! It was an accident. I was

"I'm terribly sorry but something terrible's happened,"
said Darbishire.

holding it low down and running up to do a classy backhand, when suddenly it – sort of – got caught between my knees and I tripped over and—"

"Landed up with your clumsy great elephant's hoof bang through my racket strings."

"More or less. They must have been really feeble or they'd never have bust. I didn't mean to, of course. It was just that I lost my balance and—"

"All right, all right. You needn't make speeches about it," Jennings broke in. It was no great loss really, he thought, for his racket had been in little better condition than his friend's ill-fated piece of equipment. "So long as you didn't do it for revenge."

"As though I would! I can *prove* it was an accident," Darbishire protested. "I can call vital witnesses. Ask Temple, ask Venables, ask Atkinson! They'll give evidence on oath, if necessary."

The vital witnesses, on their way upstairs to the dormitory, were close enough to hear their names being mentioned.

"That's quite right, Jen," Venables confirmed. "Darbi nearly passed out when he saw what he'd done. He said he'd buy you a new one."

"A new second-hand one," Darbishire put in quickly.

"Why bother? They've both bust each other's rackets, so why not call it quits?" Atkinson suggested.

But this easy solution didn't suit Jennings, who pointed out that such an arrangement would mean that neither of them could play tennis any more. Was it fair, he argued, to blight the hopes of two promising players who, even though they might never play at Wimbledon, could always be relied upon to make up a four on the junior court!

"We'll leave it as we arranged," he decided. "I buy Darbi a racket, and he buys me one."

"You've got a hope," said Temple. "Rackets don't grow on trees, you know. Where do you think you're going to buy a couple of second-hand ones in this part of the world?"

Neither of the donors had thought of that, but Jennings dismissed the problem with a wave of his hand.

"That's easy," he said, leading the way up to the dormitory. "I shall buy Darbi's at the same shop that he buys me mine."

"Me too," said Darbishire, following his leader up the stairs. "I'll do the same as old Jennings."

Chapter 2

The Umpire's Decision

Bromwich was so fascinated with his miniature radio that he could hardly bear to switch it off. In the dormitory that evening he undressed to the sound of pop music and burrowed under the sheets to listen to a quiz programme. Next morning he cleaned his teeth to Mozart, conducting an invisible orchestra with his toothbrush, and ate his breakfast to a background of Beethoven, keeping time with a bent-pronged fork. As the music was inaudible to everyone but him, his antics appeared baffling to those seated around him.

Wisely, he decided not to wear his set during morning school, but halfway through the cricket game that afternoon he came up to Jennings who had just returned to the scorer's box after completing his innings.

"Hey, will you look after my radio while I go in to bat?" he asked. "It's not safe to wear it with old Rumbelow bowling his ferocious leg-breaks."

"Well, I'm supposed to be umpiring by rights, but I expect they'll find someone else." Jennings put the radio into his blazer pocket and slipped the earphone into place. To his delight he found that the set was tuned in to a commentary on a county cricket match.

This should be worth listening to, he thought! This

would be better than standing out there in the hot sun, watching Martin-Jones bowling slow wides and Atkinson wielding his bat like a scythe. If they hadn't got an umpire, that was their bad luck. He'd do his turn later!

The rule about umpiring junior cricket caused more argument than any other feature of the play. The master in charge had to keep his eye on three separate games in different parts of the field. Normally, he would make his way round from pitch to pitch, leaving the game in the charge of the umpires during his absence.

Members of the batting side carried out these duties, each boy being responsible for a stint of umpiring as soon as he had finished his innings. But the task was unpopular, the batsmen preferring to watch the game from the scorer's box when they had finished facing the bowling. Thus, it was not unusual for the game to be held up from time to time while the players argued amongst themselves about who was due to take charge at the wicket. Unwilling umpires hoping to evade their duties would sometimes be found hiding in the bushes in the hope that someone else would be conscripted in their place.

Mr Wilkins was in charge of cricket that afternoon. He was a large man with a booming voice and a short supply of patience. Though fond of the boys in his charge, he could never quite understand the way in which their minds appeared to work. To L.P. Wilkins Esq, MA (Cantab) the things boys said, and the things boys did, seemed beyond the comprehension of right-thinking grown-ups.

His opinion of the antics of the rising generation was confirmed when he reached the pitch at the far end of the playing-field on his tour of supervision.

The game had come to a standstill: some of the fielders were sitting on the grass, others were practising karate or staging caterpillar races in the outfield. Two boys were fencing with uprooted stumps, and the wicket-keeper was shuffling round with his feet tucked into his gloves. The only visible umpire had made himself a pair of tight woollen trousers by forcing his legs through the arms of a long-sleeved sweater which had been placed in his care.

Mr Wilkins was horrified. "What in the name of thunder do you boys think you're doing!" he stormed, as he strode in from the boundary. "I've never seen such a disgraceful exhibition in my life."

Hurriedly, the fielders jumped to their feet and abandoned their capers. The stumps were replaced and the wicket-keeping gloves restored to their rightful limbs. The solitary umpire was less fortunate: unable to withdraw his feet through the tight wrist-bands, he hopped first on one leg, then on the other, trying to wriggle himself free from the garment clinging about his ankles.

"What's going on here? Why have you stopped playing?" the master demanded.

"We've only got one umpire, sir," said Martin-Jones, indicating the floundering figure behind the stumps. "We haven't got anybody in charge at the other end."

"Why not?"

The fielder shrugged. "He hasn't turned up, sir. It ought to be Jennings by rights, because he's just had his innings, but nobody knows where he is."

The duty master strode off to the scorer's box to make inquiries. There was no sign of the missing umpire, although several members of his side remembered seeing him only a few minutes before.

Where on earth had the silly little boy got to? Mr Wilkins was furious! Suppose the headmaster or some visitor had witnessed the scene of chaos on the cricket pitch! Whatever would they have thought?

He was just about to send another boy on to the field to replace the absentee, when a thought struck him. The scorer's box was a wooden hut raised from the ground on brick pillars about eighteen inches high. There was ample space for a slim figure to crawl underneath and remain out of sight, yet close at hand.

Mr Wilkins stooped and glanced under the little wooden structure. His complexion turned a shade pinker as he caught sight of the fugitive lying flat on his stomach with his chin cupped in his hands.

"Jennings!" he shouted. "Come out of there at once."

The umpire crawled into the sunlight and stood up. "Sir?"

"What do you mean by hiding yourself away when you're supposed to be umpiring?"

"Sorry, sir. I wasn't actually hiding, though: I just wanted to find somewhere peaceful and quiet where I could—" Jennings broke off. To reveal the reason why he needed solitude might lead to the confiscation of the radio set. "I was going to do my umpiring later, sir."

"Do it later!" The duty master was appalled. "I never heard of such a thing! The game has come to a complete stop all because of your irresponsible behaviour. And you stand there talking about peace and quiet – *tut*! What sort of peace and quiet do you think I found out there on the pitch, when I came to see how the game was getting on!"

"Sorry, sir," the culprit mumbled.

Mr Wilkins pointed to the field of play. "Off you go and get on with your job. And, what's more, you can stay out there umpiring for the rest of the innings. That'll teach you not to shirk your responsibilities another time."

The umpire scurried off to his duties and the game was restarted. Mr Wilkins stood watching until he was satisfied that everything was going smoothly, and then strode off to see what mischief was afoot in "B" game on the other side of the field.

As he stood counting the balls, Jennings was struck by the fact that Mr Wilkins hadn't noticed the pocket radio which had been relaying its programme into his right ear while he was listening to the master's tirade with the other. The information might well come in useful, for it proved that the set was inaudible to everyone but its operator, and that earpiece and lead were unlikely to be detected by casual observation.

Rumbelow, trundling up to the wicket to bowl his leg-breaks, was unaware that the umpire was controlling one game while listening to another. Indeed, Jennings became so engrossed in the broadcast cricket commentary that only half his mind was free to follow the play on the junior pitch.

Rumbelow bowled nine balls and then turned to the umpire in puzzled wonder. "Hey, isn't it about time you called *Over*?" he suggested.

"Oh yes, sorry," the umpire confessed. But five minutes later he was again following the fortunes of his favourite county side at a critical stage of their match . . .

Rumbelow bowled an easy lob, wide of the wicket, and

Atkinson poked at it with his usual scythe-like stroke, completely missing the ball which ended up against the wicket-keeper's pads.

"Out! . . . He's out!" Jennings cried excitedly.

Batsmen and fielders stared at him in astonishment.

"*Out?*" Rumbelow was flabbergasted. "*How* was he out?"

"LBW," the umpire announced.

"But it never even touched me!" Atkinson protested. "It was miles wide of my legs – wide of the stumps too."

With an effort Jennings forced his mind back to the game on hand. "It's all right, Atki, I didn't mean you."

"Yes, you did. You said I was LBW. I heard you."

"Ah, but I wasn't talking about you. I meant this bloke playing for Sussex."

"What bloke playing for Sussex?"

The situation was becoming confused, so Jennings produced the radio set from his blazer pocket and held it up for all to see. "It's old Bromo's really, but I'm looking after it until he's had his innings," he explained.

Again the game came to a stop with batsmen and fielders crowding round the umpire to inspect the set at close quarters. A chosen few were permitted to listen to snatches of the commentary before the earphone was torn from their grasp and handed over to the next listener in the queue.

Bromwich, the anxious owner, came running on to the field to make sure his property was not being mishandled.

"That's mine. Give it here!" he ordered, disentangling

the lead from Martin-Jones' grasp. "I asked Jennings to look after it – not to give everybody a free listen. I shan't get my innings before stumps are drawn at this rate."

Jennings was reluctant to part with his aid to livelier umpiring. "Well, will you lend it to me some other time, then?"

"Yes, all right. Provided I'm not using it."

"Thanks! You see, I've just had a brilliant brainwave about what we could do with it," Jennings went on. "We'd have to keep it a secret from Old Wilkie, of course, but what I thought was, how would it be if—"

But at that moment Rumbelow announced, "Hey, watch it! Old Wilkie's got us in his gun-sights."

The players scuttled to their places, aware that the duty master had a reputation for identifying culprits at a distance of two hundred yards. The game started again and Jennings, now mindful of his duties, forgot all about his brilliant brainwave by the end of the first over.

Indeed, it was not until some weeks later that he gave further thought to the question of using the pocket radio for the plan he had in mind.

Each morning at breakfast for the next few days, Darbishire reminded Jennings of his promise to replace the broken racket. And each morning Jennings parried the reminder by saying, "I haven't had a chance yet: and anyway you're supposed to be buying me one too, don't forget!"

By Saturday he had thought of an answer – not a very plausible one, but good enough to keep Darbishire quiet for the rest of the meal.

"Matron says I've got to go into Dunhambury for a

tusk inspection on Monday," he announced as he sat at Form Three table waiting for his bacon and fried bread. "I don't suppose I shall be in the dentist's for more than a few minutes, so I'll pop into that sports shop in the High Street while I'm waiting for the bus back."

"Lucky old you!" said Venables from across the table. "I've got to wait till the last week of term before I get my fangs polished."

It may seem surprising that a routine visit to the dentist should be looked upon as something of a treat by the boys of Linbury Court; but this was because a dental inspection bestowed on them the freedom of a bus journey into Dunhambury on their own. This was a rare occurrence during term time, for, apart from the Sunday afternoon walk, the boys were seldom allowed outside the school grounds unaccompanied by a master.

But dental inspections were not subject to school rules and, once away from the premises, the patient could use his appointment as an excuse to cover his activities for the rest of the afternoon. Indeed, by careful planning, the six-monthly inspection of a boy's molars and incisors could be raised to the level of an enjoyable outing.

"Are you sure you'll have time?" Darbishire asked, frowning into his teacup. "You'll have to give them a good going-over before you buy them, you know. I don't want a racket that falls to bits the first time I use it."

"Don't worry. I shall have masses of time," Jennings assured him. "I can miss the four o'clock bus even without trying, and if I accidentally on purpose manage to miss the next two as well, there won't be another bus back till half-past five."

"Right-o then," Darbishire agreed. "Only mind you don't come back without them!"

Chapter 3

Sale Price

Despite his high hopes, Jennings' excursion to Dunhambury on the following Monday did not work out at all according to plan.

During break that morning he learned that Matron had also arranged for Atkinson to have a dental inspection at the same time, so the two boys were able to travel into town together on the same bus.

"Bags I go in first when it's our turn," Jennings said, as they sat in the waiting-room thumbing through out-of-date magazines. "I've got a job to do when I come out."

Atkinson agreed with a nod. "Suits me! I'm only going to mooch round the town till I've missed a few buses. If I get back too early I might be in time for Old Wilkie's maths lesson." He shivered in mock horror at the prospect. "What's this famous job you've got lined up, then?"

"Old Darbi. I said I'd have a scout round to see if there were any second-hand rackets going begging."

"You've got a hope! Still, you never know your luck. I'll see you on the half-past five bus, then."

Jennings' visit to the surgery was a mere formality:

two minutes in the dental chair and he had passed his six-monthly inspection with nothing to worry about – apart from the dentist's usual warning to cut down on sweets and fizzy drinks.

After that, he made his way to the sports shop in the High Street where in answer to his inquiry the assistant produced a selection of brand new, very expensive tennis rackets and laid them out on the counter.

Jennings looked at them with some misgiving. "I don't really want to buy a new one – or even a good one," he explained diffidently. "I was hoping you'd got something in the second-hand line – say, round about seventy-five pence, if possible."

"Seventy-five *pence*!" The salesman shuddered and grasped the counter for support. "Seventy-five pence for a *tennis racket*!"

"Well, only an old one, of course," the customer conceded. "It doesn't matter if one or two strings are a bit wobbly, because my friend's tennis is so hopeless that he'd be just as well off with a fly-swatter really, but I said I'd try to . . ." He tailed off into silence at the sight of the pained expression on the face of the young man behind the counter.

Politely but firmly, the salesman pointed out that high-class shops specializing in the sale of sporting equipment of the finest quality could hardly be expected to stock second-hand goods. Indeed, his disdainful expression implied that he, personally, would rather be found dead in a ditch than soil his fingers with a tatty old seventy-five pence racket with wobbly strings.

"Well, do you know of any other shop where I could try?" Jennings asked.

The young assistant's shrug seemed to suggest that

second-hand tennis rackets were not the sort of thing that people bought in shops: second-hand tennis rackets were the sort of thing that people just happened to come across in the cupboard under the stairs.

Disappointed, the customer left the shop and walked on down the High Street. From what the salesman had said, it was obvious that his quest was hopeless and that he might just as well catch the next bus back to school.

But to do this would not only be an admission of failure: it would also be a shameful waste of an hour's freedom. Nobody ever caught the next bus back after a visit to the dentist – well, nobody but a clodpoll! The very idea was too clodpoll-ish for serious consideration.

So, with an hour or more to spare, Jennings left the High Street with its supermarkets and car show-rooms and wandered down the narrow streets towards the railway station. Here the shops were small and rather dingy – Upholsterers, Ironmongers, Sign-writers and Shoe Repairs *While-U-Wait*.

The cattle market stood lifeless and empty, and there was nothing to look at but brick walls and lines of parked cars all the way along to the station approach. Jennings was about to turn back when, at the next corner, he came across a shabby, single-storey building which looked to him like some sort of warehouse.

Its wide double doors were standing open and a knot of people were grouped on the pavement outside studying the pages of a typewritten catalogue. Above the entrance a faded signboard announced in letters of peeling paint: "Dunhambury Auction Mart and Sale-Rooms".

Glancing inside, Jennings saw a small crowd drifting about among the stacks of furniture which lined the walls and obstructed the gangways. At the far end, a fat man seated at a table on a rostrum was calling out figures and prices in a rapid monologue.

Jennings strolled inside to hear what the fat man was talking about.

"Four pounds, I'm bid," he was declaiming, as Jennings edged his way into the group of purchasers. "Four pounds, twenty-five . . . four pounds, fifty. Any advance on four-fifty? . . . Four-seventy-five . . . five pounds. Going at five pounds . . . going . . . gone!"

The auctioneer rapped on the table with his gavel and turned to the next item on his list. "Lot 83. Genuine antique marble washstand. Who'll start the bidding at ten pounds?"

For a while Jennings stood watching and listening with the half-hearted curiosity of one who has nothing better to do. It was the first time he had been to an auction sale and, from what he could see of it, it did not look a very exciting form of entertainment. The goods on display were either so old-fashioned or so useless that he would not have taken them as a gift – let alone bid for them in competition with rival bargain-hunters.

Who, for example, would want that worm-eaten wickerwork rocking chair (Lot 64) over by the window? Or the fly-blown mirror in the chipped gilt frame (Lot 67) that was standing beside it? He'd never seen such a load of old rubbish. Mildly curious, he began to make his way round the piles of junk, but to begin with he could find nothing that seemed worth a second glance.

Then, in the gangway on the far side of the sale-room, he came across a number of tea-chests and cardboard cartons containing oddly-assorted articles. Lot 92, for instance, consisted of a pair of kitchen scales, a portable record-player and a string hammock. Lot 93 in the adjoining box consisted of a sewing-machine, a dartboard and a folding canvas stool.

What were such ill-assorted objects doing in the same container, he wondered? Perhaps they were selling the entire contents of a house and these domestic odds and ends had come to light in the attic – or in the cupboard under the stairs!

What else was there? With luck, some dust-encrusted bargain might be lying at the bottom of one of the tea-chests.

He continued his search. There was Lot 95 – hot-water bottles and hockey sticks. Lot 96 – a faded oil painting and a camp cooking-stove. Lot 97 – a coal scuttle, a dog's overcoat and—!

Jennings' eyes opened wide in surprise; for there in the tea-chest beside the coal scuttle and the dog's overcoat were two old tennis rackets!

It was unbelievable! It was too good to be true! All he need do was to buy Lot 97 when it came up for sale, and he and Darbishire could repay their debt to each other as agreed. Provided, of course, that the bidding was within his price range.

How long would it be before Lot 97 came under the hammer, he wondered? Jennings glanced up at the rostrum and found to his surprise that the auctioneer had disposed of all the articles of furniture and was about to start selling the oddments in the tea-chests.

"Lot 92 – miscellaneous collection of household and garden objects," the fat man announced, looking up from his list. "A real treasure trove of useful domestic appliances! Now, who'll start the bidding?"

He signalled to the sale-room porter to display the

contents of the tea-chest. But this turned out to be an unwise move, for when the objects were held aloft the arm dropped off the portable record-player and the string hammock was so coated with mildew that the porter was unable to unroll it. There was no bid for this treasure trove of old rubbish and the auctioneer hurriedly passed on to Lot 93.

This time he had better luck, for two young housewives were both so anxious to secure the sewing-machine that they raised their bids to six pounds before one of them dropped out of the contest.

Jennings listened with growing alarm as the bidding soared upwards. Six pounds – *Wow*! . . . He could not possibly compete with wealthy grown-ups prepared to spend such fantastic sums of money. He had precisely seventy-five pence in addition to his bus fare. What chance had he of securing Lot 97 in the teeth of such tough opposition?

On the other hand, he didn't want to buy the entire contents of the tea-chest: this would be a waste of money when all he needed were the tennis rackets. So would the auctioneer agree to sell the items separately, he wondered? That would get rid of the coal scuttle enthusiasts and the dog's overcoat fanciers, leaving him with a good chance of snapping up the rackets at a bargain price.

It was worth trying, and certainly there would be no harm in asking. But he'd have to be quick, for already Lot 96 was coming under the hammer, and the porter was holding up the oil painting and the cooking-stove that made up the consignment on offer.

"Lot 96 – paraffin cooking-stove," the auctioneer read from his list. "Also, painting entitled *Country*

Scene in Spring, artist unknown, fifteen inches by eight."
He looked hopefully around the audience. "What am I
bid? . . . Two pounds? . . . Who'll start me off with two
pounds for the two?"

The suggestion was received in chilly silence. "One
pound fifty pence then? . . . What, no bid at one fifty!
Come along now," the fat man urged. "You may be
missing the chance of a lifetime . . . Hold the picture
higher, Charlie, so they can see it . . . No, no, the other
way; you've got it upside down . . . There now, ladies
and gentlemen: a genuine old master going for a song,
and a camp cooking-stove thrown in for good measure.
Who says seventy-five pence for the two?"

Jennings had no particular interest in Lot 96, but
he was anxious to know whether Lot 97 could be split
up into separate parts, so he put up his hand and said,
"Excuse me, I just wanted to ask—"

He got no further. To the auctioneer the upraised
hand was a gesture of agreement and he said, "Right!
Seventy-five pence, I'm bid. Any advance on seventy-
five pence?" A glance round the sale-room showed that
nobody else was anxious to join the bidding. "Going
at seventy-five pence . . . going . . . gone! Sold to the
young customer on my right for seventy-five pence."

It was not for some moments that Jennings realized
that, all unknowingly, he had become the legal owner of
Lot 96. The first indication that something unexpected
had happened was the arrival of Charlie, the sale-room
porter, who marched up to him and dumped the cooking-
stove and the painting down on a marble washstand on
which Jennings had perched himself.

"Seventy-five pence, please, son," he said, holding
out his hand for the money.

Jennings stared at him in astonishment. "But these aren't mine. I didn't buy them. I didn't even bid for them," he protested.

"Don't come that lark with me," the man replied. "Of course you bid for them. You put your hand up and called out. I heard you."

"Ah yes, but that was because I wanted to ask a question. I wanted to know if those tennis rackets in Lot 97—"

"Who's talking about Lot 97! Lot 96, this is." The porter was a large, red-faced man in a brown overall with a pencil tucked behind one ear and a half-smoked cigarette lodged behind the other. Clearly, he had no time to waste on defaulting customers and little sympathy with youngsters who were unfamiliar with the rules and practice of the sale-room. "Come along now, son. Pay up sharp and take the stuff away. I've got a lot of work to get through this afternoon."

"But I didn't mean to buy them. It was a mistake," the customer insisted. "This old junk is no use to me."

His protest was overheard by an elderly woman trundling a recently purchased tea-trolley along the gangway. She came to rest beside the marble washstand, and stared hard at the faded painting.

"I'd hang on to that picture, if I were you," she advised. "For all you know it might be one of those valuable old masters – worth a fortune, some of them!"

"It doesn't look valuable to me," Jennings complained. For a moment he wondered whether she would agree to buy it for seventy-five pence, but before he could make the suggestion she went on, "You keep it, son. Don't you part with it! I was reading in the paper only the other day about some man picking up a painting on the cheap and it turned out to be an old master, worth thousands of pounds."

Nodding her head to underline the wisdom of her words, she passed on down the gangway, leaving Jennings to the mercy of the porter who, fretting with impatience, was still holding out his hand for the money.

It would be useless to argue, Jennings decided, though he bitterly resented the auctioneer taking advantage of his inexperience. Unwillingly, he fumbled in his pocket and handed over seventy-five pence. Then he picked up his unwanted purchases and made his way out into the afternoon sunshine.

The 5.30 pm double-decker Southdown to Linbury was standing empty in the bus station when Jennings arrived some twenty minutes before the time of departure. He climbed aboard and took a front seat on the upper deck. Then, to while away the time of waiting, he began a half-hearted inspection of his newly acquired possessions.

The camp cooking-stove was a bargain, he decided: or rather it *would* have been if he had wanted a camp cooking-stove – which he didn't! It was a simple gadget consisting of a boiling ring surrounding a gauze pad which, in turn, was connected to a paraffin fuel tank. Without cooking utensils it was useless, he thought – except, perhaps, as a present for Darbishire to make up for the racket which would now have to be written off as a dead loss.

After that he looked at the oil painting, but there

was nothing about it to excite his imagination. As far as he could see it was just a rather drab picture of a thatched cottage with a milkmaid in eighteenth-century dress carrying a pail and a three-legged stool down the garden path. In the middle distance a shepherd in a smock was keeping half an eye on his sheep while practising what appeared to be a descant recorder.

It certainly didn't look like a priceless old master, worth thousands of pounds: it didn't even look worth the seventy-five pence that he had been obliged to pay for it. He sighed and shook his head. Fossilised fish-hooks! What a muddle it had all been! And even now he didn't know what had happened to Lot 97 and the two tennis rackets that had been the cause of all the trouble!

By this time the top deck was filling up, and soon afterwards the bell rang and the bus started on its journey. As it did so, another passenger arrived at the top of the stairs; immediately there was a shout of recognition and Jennings heard somebody calling his name in a shrill treble. Glancing round, he saw Atkinson advancing along the gangway towards him, beaming with triumph and carrying two old tennis rackets.

"How about these, then!" the late-comer cried, waving his trophies like semaphore flags. "Just what you want, aren't they?"

Jennings stared at him in puzzled wonder. "Where on earth did you get them from?"

"Aha! You'd like to know, wouldn't you! Well, it was just a lucky chance, really."

The bus turned the corner into the High Street, sending Atkinson lurching sideways to collapse on the knees of his travelling companion. Recovering, he settled himself on the adjoining seat, to the relief of nearby passengers who had narrowly avoided being scalped by the flailing tennis rackets.

"Well, I'd got nothing special to do when I came out of the dentist's so I went to a tea-shop called Ye Olde Tudor Bunne Shoppe and had an olde Tudor bunne." Atkinson paused and shook his head at the memory. "I reckon they ought to call it Ye Olde Tudor Cement Works: my bun was so hard that I nearly went back to the dentist's again to see if my teeth had come unstuck at the roots."

This was hardly the moment, Jennings felt, to waste time listening to a minute-by-minute account of Atkinson's social activities. "You can skip all that part," he broke in impatiently. "Where did you find these rackets?"

"I was coming to that. Well, after my tea-break I mooched back to the bus station along a side street I hadn't been down before. And after a bit I came across this warehouse sort of place with the doors open and a lot of people coming away."

Jennings looked at him sharply. "Was it called the Dunhambury Auction Mart?"

"Something like that. How did you know?"

"Never mind that, now. What happened then?"

The facts were easily explained. Arriving by chance outside the auction rooms just as the sale had finished, Atkinson had seen the porter dumping the unsold junk on the pavement for collection by the corporation refuse lorry. Clearly, Lot 97 had failed to find a purchaser, for amongst the remains had been a tea-chest containing a dog's overcoat, a coal scuttle and two old tennis rackets.

"As soon as I saw them I thought to myself, 'Aha!' I thought. 'Old Jen's on the look-out for a couple of those,' " Atkinson went on. "So I asked this bloke in the overalls if I could have them, and he said anybody could take the whole boiling lot for all he cared."

"What – free of charge?"

"Yes, why not! They'd have gone straight into the dustcart if I hadn't salvaged them."

Jennings heard the explanation with mixed feelings. Delighted though he was at Atkinson's easy success, he felt even more incensed to think that his own efforts had ended in such dismal failure. It was most unfair! And to make matters worse, the rackets now belonged to Atkinson who had done so little to deserve them.

"I thought you might like to buy them," Atkinson went on, as though reading Jennings' thoughts. "Ever so cheap, of course. I don't want to make much profit. How about seventy-five pence for the two?"

"But I haven't got seventy-five pence left, now – thanks to that stupid porter." Jennings flipped his fingers with frustration. "What you don't know is that I went there myself and tried to buy them, only something went wrong and I came out with an old master by mistake."

"Came out with an old master?" Atkinson looked puzzled. "One of *our* masters, do you mean? I didn't know any of them were in Dunhambury this afternoon."

"Not an old *school*master – an old *painting* master," Jennings replied irritably. He picked up the canvas from the floor and thrust it into his companion's hand. "Here you are. I'll swop you this for those two rackets!"

Atkinson didn't think much of the picture. He wrinkled his nose and said, "Somebody's spilt gravy powder all over it."

"That's just because it's old. You can easily clean it

up a bit with an india-rubber," Jennings informed him. "Actually, you'd be getting a terrific bargain. Somebody told me it might be worth thousands of pounds, some day."

There was a pause while Atkinson considered the offer. Then he said, "I'd rather settle for seventy-five pence now, and be sure of it."

They were still haggling over the so-called bargain when the bus stopped outside the school gates, and it was not until they were halfway up the drive that the terms were agreed upon.

Then Jennings said, "Well, all right then. I'll get Darbishire to pay you the seventy-five pence out of his pocket money, and I'll give him the picture to make up for it." He grinned. "Lucky old Darbi! He may be a millionaire if it turns out to be an old master."

Atkinson snorted and said, "Huh! He's welcome. What with Mr Carter on at me about my English prep and Old Wilkie moaning about my maths, I've got enough old masters to be going on with, thanks very much."

Chapter 4

The Hide-out

The tea bell was ringing as Jennings and Atkinson reached the school buildings, so there was no time for Jennings to do anything but leave his new possessions in the basement and hurry off to the dining-hall.

Darbishire was anxious to know whether his friend had had any luck. All through tea he kept asking questions, but amidst the clamour of conversation at the third-form table, he was unable to make much sense of Jennings' references to paraffin stoves, dogs' overcoats, surly men in overalls and elderly female art experts wheeling tea-trolleys. However, after the meal was over, his friend took him along to the shoe-room to see for himself the results of the afternoon's excursion.

Darbishire was delighted with the rackets and agreed to pay the seventy-five pence demanded, provided that he was allowed to choose which of the two should be his. This led to an argument, as one of the rackets was in better condition than the other, and eventually the matter was settled by the toss of a coin.

"I don't want that tatty old picture, though," he demurred, when Jennings offered him the so-called old master as part of the bargain. "Why can't I have the cooking-stove instead?"

"All right, then – you can!" Jennings could afford to be generous, having won the toss and chosen the better racket for himself. "What are you going to use it for?"

Darbishire scratched his nose thoughtfully. He had no clear ideas on the subject, but he felt that he ought to offer some sort of suggestion to justify his claim. So he said, "Well, it's a camping stove, by rights. So what I thought was, I could do some camp cookery on it, if only we'd got a camp to do it in. And something to cook, of course. You know, fried sausages and that sort of thing."

Vague and hazy though the notion was, Jennings seized upon it with enthusiasm. "Not a bad idea, Darbi," he said, his mind shaping the hazy notion into a workable plan. "We could get round Mrs Hackett to give us some bacon or sausages or something from the kitchen."

"We haven't got a frying-pan, though."

"So what! We can easily make one out of a tin lid."

"And paraffin?"

"No problem! Robinson's got some in the tool shed: he uses it for his bonfires." Jennings paused to consider the practical difficulties. Robinson, the school cleaner and odd-job man, regarded boys with mistrust and could seldom be relied upon to play his part in schemes demanding his co-operation.

"Perhaps we could chat him up a bit. You know, offer to tidy the shed for him and all that flannel. He couldn't refuse us a titchy little bottle of paraffin if we went out of our way to be nice to him, could he!"

Darbishire began to look interested. So far the plan seemed feasible, but there was one important item which hadn't yet been touched upon. "That's all very well," he said, "but you seem to forget that we haven't *got* a camp to do the cooking in."

"Not yet, we haven't," Jennings conceded. "Just give me a chance to process the data in my think-tank. I'll soon come up with an idea."

The bell rang for evening prep. Jennings put the faded *Country Scene in Spring* in his tuck-box while Darbishire concealed the cooking-stove behind the shoe-lockers. The tennis rackets were left on the window sill, ready for a quick getaway to the junior court as soon as prep was over.

"We'll make it a secret camp site," Jennings decided, as they hurried up the stairs to Form Three classroom. "Nobody's to know where it is in case the masters find out and stop us, so mind you don't go round telling people."

"How can I tell anyone when I don't know where it is myself?" Darbishire demanded. "I suppose you're just going to stick a pin in a map of the world and say, 'OK, we'll build it on top of Mount Everest!' "

"Not exactly!" Jennings frowned, and led the way into the classroom. "Actually, Darbi, I *have* got an idea, but you'll have to wait till Sunday before we can do anything about it."

The Sunday afternoon walk was the only regular occasion on which the boys of Linbury Court were allowed outside the grounds by themselves – and even this concession did not apply to the lowest forms who set out when Sunday lunch was over in the charge of the master on duty.

In pairs, or groups of three or four, the boys in the middle and upper forms were free to make their way through the surrounding countryside, exploring the byways leading up to the South Downs, or wandering at will along the footpaths across neighbouring farmland and through the overgrown copses of Miller's Wood.

Clearly then, Sunday was the only suitable day on which to look for a camp site, Jennings explained to Darbishire after prep that evening, as they waited for their turn to use the tennis court. Meanwhile, they could spend their free time in improvising a few simple cooking pots and trying to find suitable food to cook in them.

With this in mind, Jennings hung about outside the school kitchen at break next morning, hoping to persuade one of the domestic staff to provision the camp larder for them. Unfortunately, Mrs Hackett was too busy preparing the lunch to listen properly: misunderstanding his needs, she assumed that he wanted to replenish the scraps on the bird-table and gave him a bag of old toast crusts and bacon rinds left over from breakfast.

Meanwhile, Darbishire was making a saucepan out of a cocoa tin and straightening the prongs of an old fork that he had found in the long grass behind the cricket pavilion. But the cocoa tin leaked like a colander when he tested it, and two of the prongs broke off the fork as he was bending them into shape in the jamb of the common-room door.

It was not a very encouraging start: and a further set-back occurred that evening when Robinson told them that the tool shed didn't need tidying and that, anyway, he had no paraffin to spare.

On Thursday, during cricket practice, when they were bemoaning their lack of progress, Jennings said, "It doesn't really matter, Darbi, because we can't actually *do* any cooking until we've got our camp properly set up. That's going to take all our time on Sunday afternoon, so we'd better leave the cooker behind until we're ready for it."

Darbishire agreed. He was already growing worried about the problem of smuggling the stove off the premises. It wasn't the sort of apparatus that he could tuck up his sweater when setting off down the drive under the watchful eye of the master on duty.

Mr Carter was the duty master on Sunday afternoon. Jennings and Darbishire gave their names to him in the staff-room after lunch, and then set out on their quest.

Their way led across the playing fields and out through the bottom gate at the far end of the school grounds. From here they followed the footpath across the fields past Arrowsmith's farm, skirting Linbury village away to their left and Miller's Wood on their right. In less than a mile the footpath became a mere track, and then petered out altogether on the steeply rising slope of the South Downs.

They were still on farmland, but now the soil was chalky and crops gave way to sheep grazing on the coarse, springy turf. Prickly gorse bushes grew in little forests, scratching the skin and tearing the clothes of anyone rash enough to force an entry. Beyond the bushes, the slopes rose to a summit of rough grass which extended half a mile or more before reaching the sheer drop down to the sea.

This was the territory that Jennings had in mind

as being the right sort of place to set up camp. It was off the route of the usual Sunday walks, but he remembered it from a school picnic the previous summer, when Mr Carter had organized lively games of hide-and-seek amongst the gorse bushes.

"There's a place somewhere over there that'd be just the thing," he said, pointing to an extensive patch of uneven ground largely screened from view by undergrowth. "I took cover in there once when Bromwich and Rumbelow were chasing me, and they never did find me: it was just like the African jungle."

He led the way to the bushes which stretched a hundred yards or more in each direction. The sun was hot on their shoulders as they followed the edge of the gorse thickets until they found a small gap through which they crawled on hands and knees.

At first the going was slow, with branches brushing their faces and roots tripping their feet, but after a while they were able to walk upright, and eventually the bushes thinned out and they found themselves in a clearing. On one side the ground fell away steeply to a valley some distance below; on the other side a tall bank stretched up like a miniature cliff, disappearing in a clump of bushes which cut off the crest of the hill from their line of vision.

Darbishire gazed about him in wonder and delight. "Wow! It's fantastic! There couldn't be anywhere better. And it's ever so secret. Nobody would ever find a camp hidden away in a spot like this."

Jennings nodded in agreement. "It's even better than I thought. I didn't come as far as this last summer, but I could tell it was the sort of place we wanted."

"I can just see it when it's finished," Darbishire went

on, gazing about him in excited anticipation. "Me doing the cooking on my little stove: sausages sizzling, bacon crackling, cocoa bubbling away like nobody's business; and – you – er . . . " What could Jennings be doing? "Well, you could wash up afterwards, while I sit back playing camp-fire songs on my recorder."

"Thanks very much," Jennings said curtly. "What you seem to forget is that we've got to build the camp first and we haven't even thought how we're going to do it, yet."

They squatted on the grass and argued the matter out in some detail. At first, they agreed that the camp should be a hut of some sort, made from foliage growing close at hand. But should they build it from branches and thatch it with brushwood, or would it be better to tunnel directly into a clump of gorse and hollow out the interior to an acceptable shape?

"Either way, we shall need tools," Darbishire pointed out, after the discussion had gone full circle. "Say, for instance, a saw and an axe and a spade and a pair of shears and—"

"Why not a bulldozer and a cement-mixer while you're about it!" Jennings suggested. "You know perfectly well we haven't a hope of getting hold of tools like that – let alone lugging them all the way up here without anybody knowing."

"Well, *you* think of something better, then!" Darbishire rolled over on his stomach and mopped his forehead. Although the gorse around them was dense and shady, the high afternoon sun beat down into the clearing from a clear blue sky. From the summit of the Downs above them they could hear the distant bleating of Mr Arrowsmith's sheep.

Jennings got up and turned to face the cliff-like gradient behind them. "We must do *something*," he said. "We can't just sit here wasting all afternoon arguing about—" He stopped in mid-sentence staring intently at the rising slope. Twenty yards higher up the bank, a geological fault in the chalk subsoil had resulted in the formation of an opening in the hillside. It was in shadow and he could not see how deeply it penetrated, but at least it looked worth investigating. "Hey, Darbi, look up there!" he said.

"I'm too hot. I shall melt if I move. What is it?"

"I'm not sure, but it looks like a little cave. Come on, let's go and make an inspection. It might be just what we're looking for."

"I bet it isn't. I bet it's nothing at all really. You're always seeing things that aren't there."

Grumbling, Darbishire struggled to his feet and followed his companion who was already clambering up the slope on hands and knees. Seconds later, they reached the fault in the rock and found themselves staring into the shadowy gloom of a cavern disappearing into the chalk.

"How about this, then!" Jennings' eyes sparkled with triumph. "It solves the whole problem: no tools required. We've found a ready-made camp just waiting for us to move in."

Darbishire laughed excitedly. "Cave-dwellers – that's us! We could be prehistoric cavemen with clubs, hunting dinosaurs for our food."

"You'd have a job cooking a dinosaur on your tatty old paraffin stove," Jennings told him.

He knelt in the entrance and peered in. The opening was a mere hole in the hillside, too low to allow him to stand upright. Once over the threshold, however, there was ample headroom and the cave became a rough triangle with a base of ten feet at its widest point, just inside the cave mouth. The side walls converged towards the apex to form a narrow passage leading farther into the hill where not even the faintest shaft of daylight could penetrate.

Jennings and Darbishire crawled through the opening and stood up, looking about them. Floor, walls and roof were composed of chalk: only round the entrance was there a deposit of reddish-brown soil on which coarse grass grew in tufts and little pink flowers struggled to maintain a root-hold.

Darbishire's lively imagination got to work at once. "Wow! Perhaps it's a smugglers' cave," he hazarded, staring at the crevice leading into the rock. "If we crawled along there we might find it crammed with things like, say, for instance, old oak chests full of contraband brandy and rum and stuff."

"They don't smuggle things like that these days," Jennings said, bringing his friend back into the twentieth century. "Nowadays, it's all watches and cameras and microfilm and things." He moved across to the passage and poked his head in. "Can't see a thing! Looks too damp for smugglers, though. Who'd want an old oak chest full of rusty watches and mouldy cameras!"

It was cold in the cave after the hot sun outside and he turned back with a shiver. "First of all we must find out how far in that tunnel goes, but we can't do a thing without a torch."

Darbishire glanced at his watch. "And, anyway, we can't stop now. It's half-past four already. Time we were off, if we're not going to be late back."

"W.ow! Perhaps it's a smugglers' cave," said Darbishire.

They crawled back into the sunlight and slithered from the cave entrance to the point halfway down the bank where they had first entered the clearing. It was heavy-going, trudging through the undergrowth to the downland beyond. As they went, they could hear the cry of gulls mingling with the occasional bleating of the grazing sheep.

They had nearly reached open country when they heard a loud scuffling sound away to their left.

"What's that?" Jennings said, stopping abruptly. They both stood still listening as the noise continued.

"Rabbits?" Darbishire suggested.

"Don't be stupid. From the row it's kicking up, it sounds more like one of your famous prehistoric dinosaurs."

Curious, they picked their way across in the direction of the sound and quite soon they came across an old Southdown ewe struggling to free its head from under the bole of an elder tree which had been uprooted across its path. There was a patch of juicy foliage on the far side, just out of reach, which suggested that the animal had been trying unsuccessfully to squeeze its way under the branch in search of food.

"Silly old sheep, you're pulling the wrong way," Jennings said. But the animal, panicking now at the boys' approach, continued to get its neck stuck even more tightly between the branch and the ground.

Jennings took hold of one end of the branch and heaved. "Don't just stand there, Darbi. Come and help me!"

Between them they managed to raise the branch about six inches. As the pressure was relieved the sheep shot out backwards, turned, and rushed off to join the others on the open grassland.

"It didn't even stop to say thank you," Darbishire complained. "Never mind, we've got a good excuse now for being late."

They ran all the way to the foot of the Downs and reached the footpath crossing Arrowsmith's farm. Passing a field gate, they caught sight of the farmer who waved vaguely as they came into view. Mr Arrowsmith was on nodding terms with all the Linbury boys, though it was doubtful whether he knew any of them by name. The boys, for their part, dutifully raised their caps whenever they happened to meet him.

Jennings came to a stop by the gate and said, "Excuse me, Mr Arrowsmith, we've just rescued one of your sheep. It had got its head stuck under a branch up on the Downs."

"That was good of you," the farmer replied. "There's one pig-headed old ewe up there who's always doing things like that. We call her Mrs Maverick because she's a bit of a rover. She doesn't seem to have heard of the rule that sheep are supposed to stay in the flock and follow the leader." He laughed aloud at his little joke. "I expect my sheep-looker would have spotted something was wrong when he went up there this evening, but thanks all the same."

It was a few minutes past five by the school clock when Jennings and Darbishire slipped into the building by the side door and hurried along to the staff-room to report their return to Mr Carter.

"You're late," the master informed them from his armchair, laying aside the Sunday paper. "Not *very* late, as it happens, so I might even have overlooked the matter, but for the fact that you appear to have been caught up in an earthquake."

They glanced down at their clothes, only now aware of the chalk and soil streaking their garments from shoulder to ankle. Burrs were sticking to their socks, odd stalks of grass adhered to their sweaters. The toes of their shoes were scuffed white and the seats of their trousers bore the marks of the slither down the hill.

"Sorry, sir," Jennings apologized, making futile brushing movements down the front of his sweater. "We – er – we found a sheep, you see, and it had got stuck, so we rescued it."

Mr Carter nodded. "I'm very glad to hear it. I gather, then, that you've been up on the Downs?"

For a moment Jennings hesitated. They couldn't deny the fact, but they had agreed that their camping project must be kept a secret from the masters. Playing for time, he said, "I thought we were allowed up there, sir."

"So you are: there's no rule about it," Mr Carter conceded. "I merely mention the fact because the headmaster's getting rather worried about the untidy state some of you boys are in when you come back on Sunday afternoons. He's threatening to stop you from going out by yourselves, if it continues."

"Yes, sir, sorry, sir."

"All right, then, you can run along now. I just thought a timely warning wouldn't come amiss."

Mr Carter smiled and retired behind his paper. The senior assistant master was a friendly, easy-going man with a shrewd understanding of what went on in the minds of boys in his care. For this reason they liked and respected him, looking upon him as someone in authority whom they could always trust to set right the little grievances and injustices that were so much a part of boarding-school life. Indeed, the most serious fault that could be laid at Mr Carter's door was the fact that he knew too much. However carefully a culprit might strive to conceal his misdeeds, Mr Carter usually found out in the end.

This last criticism was in Darbishire's mind as the two boys left the staff-room and went down to the washroom to get ready for tea.

"That puts the tin lid on our secret plans then," he said gloomily. "If Mr Carter's giving us a warning, it means he knows we're up to something, so it'd be asking for trouble to go off to the camp site again next Sunday."

"Of course it doesn't. He didn't say we weren't allowed to go, did he?"

"Well, no, but—"

"Well, there you are then. We'll just have to be a bit careful about looking tidy when we come back, that's all."

Jennings turned to a washbasin, trailed his fingers under the cold tap for a few seconds and then wiped the grime and the chalk off on a clean roller towel. He smiled knowingly at his companion who was searching the floor for a piece of soap. "Just do as I tell you, Darbi, and everything will be all right," he said. "There's not much anyone can teach me about keeping secrets from masters."

Chapter 5

Quiet Commentary

Form Three had a double art period with Mr Hind after break on Monday mornings. The art master (who also taught music) was a tall, pale young man who had a flair for telling such terrible jokes that his classes would wince and groan in mock agony; though, actually, the feebler the jokes the better they liked them, and the louder they would clamour for more.

For the first part of Monday's lesson, the boys busied themselves in assembling collages and modelling designs in coloured candlewax, while the master made his way round the room offering helpful advice.

Then, unexpectedly, Bromwich put up his hand and said, "Sir, please, sir, may I go and find Mr Wilkins, sir? I've just remembered I want to see him."

"What, *now*? In the middle of my lesson? Of course you can't," the master replied.

"Oh, but sir, I *must*! You see, Matron said I wasn't to play cricket today because I wasn't feeling very well: only I forgot to tell Mr Wilkins, so he'll put me down to play, and it'll be too late to stop him if I wait till after school."

"Too bad," Mr Hind sympathized. "But I'm certainly

not letting you out of my class, bothering Mr Wilkins when you're supposed to be working."

"But sir, it's urgent. I'm in a mess, sir," Bromwich pleaded. "You see, if I play this afternoon I shall get into trouble with Matron, and if I don't, I shall be in trouble with Mr Wilkins. So what shall I do, sir?"

Mr Hind shrugged. "You'll just have to choose the lesser of two evils, won't you?"

Bromwich was not familiar with the expression. "Choose the *what*, sir?" he said in puzzled tones. "I don't know what you mean."

By way of reply, Mr Hind crossed to the blackboard and with a few rapid strokes drew a picture of a large beetle waving its proboscis in the air.

The class stopped working to watch, wondering whether this might turn out to be one of Mr Hind's terrible jokes. They were right – it did!

Having completed his beetle, the artist drew an identical, but smaller, insect beside it. Then he turned to the questioner and said, "Allow me to explain, Bromwich, in words so simple that even you can understand." He pointed to his handiwork. "These creatures are both weevils – grain-eating insects which do great damage to crops. As you can see, one is larger than the other. Therefore, the smaller one is the lesser of two weevils."

The pun was greeted with the usual derision. All round the room boys groaned, sighed, winced, held their heads in their hands or collapsed in mock faints into the arms of their neighbours. A few of them, improvising weapons from pencils and rulers, polished off the joker with a burst of machine-gun fire.

Bromwich, however, was always slow to see a joke.

He continued to look puzzled, and finally said, "But, sir, I don't know where to find a weevil. And even if I *did*, I don't see how it would stop me getting into trouble with Mr Wilkins."

The remark produced a fresh outburst of merriment and it was some time before the class settled down again to work.

Soon afterwards, Bromwich was looking pale and complaining of a headache, so Mr Hind sent him to report to Matron in the dispensary. It was as well that he did so, for Matron had had doubts about the boy's fitness earlier in the day, and as he was now feeling worse and was running a slight temperature, she sent him straight to bed.

Towards the end of the period, Form Three laid aside their collages and designs, and listened while Mr Hind talked to them about the primitive cave paintings of prehistoric ages – paintings which until recent years had remained unknown and unsuspected since before the dawn of recorded time.

He told the fascinating story of the Lascaux cave paintings in France, discovered by chance when two local boys were taking their dog for a walk; and he showed them copies of the animals painted on the cave walls – simple drawings, crude in design and execution, yet regarded as priceless by reason of their antiquity.

Darbishire listened spellbound as the tale was told, his imagination fired by the thought that he and Jennings could now claim to be occupiers of a cave as remote and ancient as those that had guarded the artistic efforts of primitive man – well, *almost*! So why shouldn't he become a cave artist!

In his mind's eye he saw himself on peaceful Sunday

afternoons recording highlights of modern civilization on the walls in poster paint. In the course of time the entrance to the cave would become overgrown and his paintings buried in the hillside, to be discovered thousands of years later.

He would sign the pictures, of course, thus ensuring his future fame. Professors in the year AD 5000 would argue about the merits of a genuine Darbishire cave painting, depicting the outmoded computers and jet aircraft in use in the twentieth century. He would take his paints with him and start work next Sunday. In fact, he might even become the only artist who had ever—

"What was I saying, Darbishire?"

Mr Hind's question shattered the artist's daydream like a pistol shot.

"I – er – I beg your pardon, sir?" Darbishire stammered, trying to adjust his mind to the realities of the present day.

"Wool-gathering as usual! I should have thought that the discovery of cave art would have been interesting enough to hold your attention."

"So it is, sir. I'm terribly interested, really. It was just that I didn't quite—"

"No excuses, thank you." Mr Hind turned to the adjoining table and repeated his question. "Well, Venables, why do you think these primitive peoples felt an urge to express themselves by drawing on the walls of their caves?"

Venables frowned in thought, and then his eyes lit up with inspiration. "I suppose it was because they hadn't got proper drawing paper, sir," he said brightly.

Mr Hind took a short walk round the art-room to relieve his feelings. At times like these he wondered whether trying to teach Art to Form Three was really worth the effort!

Bromwich's illness turned out to be an attack of summer flu which kept him in the sick-room for a week. His absence coincided with the third Test Match of the season in which England were playing against the West Indies at the Old Trafford cricket ground.

As always, the Linbury boys did their best to follow the course of the match but, as so often happened on these occasions, they were frustrated by having to wait until the day's play was over before they could catch up with the state of the game. For it was not until after tea that they were allowed access to the television set in the library to hear the latest scores and – if they were lucky – to watch a brief re-run of the highlights of the play.

By Monday evening the match had reached a critical stage. England, struggling to avoid defeat, had been reprieved by a brilliant seventh-wicket stand which remained unbroken when stumps were drawn for the day. The outcome of the match hung in the balance and would certainly be decided on the following day, with everything depending upon the two batsmen in the vital partnership.

"Wow! It's going to be an exciting finish," Atkinson said, when Mr Carter switched off the set at the end of the sports programme. "I'd give anything to watch it tomorrow, wouldn't you, Temple!"

"Fat chance we've got!" Temple snorted resentfully. "It may be all over by lunch time, and we shan't even know what happened. It's really not fair," he went on, as the bell rang for prep and the crowd round the television set melted away. "What's the good of having TV if we're not allowed to watch it at the proper time!"

"You can see it tomorrow evening," Mr Carter reminded him.

"Ah yes, sir, but it'll be stale news by then. It's while it's actually happening that you want to know what's going on. Fossilised fish-hooks! If only I'd got a carrier pigeon, or something!"

Mr Carter smiled and chivvied the boys out of the library. "You be thankful for small mercies, Temple. You can hardly expect the work of the school to come to a complete stop every time there's a Test Match."

Jennings wore a satisfied smile in Dormitory Four that evening. "If we can't watch it on telly, at least we can hear the ball-by-ball commentary on radio," he told his colleagues as they undressed. "We can use Bromwich's transistor."

"Bromo's in the sick-room," Venables pointed out. "Went up this morning."

"Yes, but he hasn't taken his set with him. I saw it in his locker when I put his history book back this afternoon. And he told me weeks ago I could borrow it some time, when he wasn't using it."

At first hearing the idea sounded impractical. Atkinson said, "But if we're all in class doing maths with Old Wilkie, we can't very well be listening to the radio, can we!"

"We can on Bromo's titchy little set. I tried it out on the cricket field once while I was actually talking to Sir, and he didn't notice a thing."

Jennings' plan was simple. When play started at half-past eleven next morning, he would sit in the back row listening to the commentary, safe in the knowledge that the tiny radio would not be detected

53

by the master in charge of the class. At intervals, he would pass round scraps of paper detailing the latest score and any other snippets of information concerning the state of the game.

"It'll be all right if we're careful," he said as he explained the details of his scheme. "We'll make sure all the others know what's going on, so they don't give the game away."

As it happened, there was one serious snag about Jennings' radio news service that did not become apparent until halfway through Mr Wilkins' maths lesson the following morning.

To begin with, it was all plain sailing. Jennings retrieved the radio from Bromwich's locker during morning break, and by the time the next lesson started he was seated in his usual place with the set in his shirt pocket and the lead running up inside his blazer to the tiny earphone snuggling imperceptibly in his left ear.

Mr Wilkins noticed nothing amiss when he started his lesson; and as the class had been warned what to expect, the earlier messages passed from hand to hand without detection. The difficulty arose when the news bulletins, having traversed the room, reached the end of the line and could go no farther.

Rumbelow, seated at the end desk in the front row, found himself being snowed under with slips of paper which became more and more difficult to conceal as they continued to arrive. In desperation, he began tucking them between the pages of his maths textbook – and then looked up to find that Mr Wilkins' eye was upon him!

The master made no comment, but a few minutes later he set the class some problems to work out in their books. As soon as they were all at work, he strolled along the front row till he reached Rumbelow's desk. Stretching out his hand, he removed a slip of paper from the textbook. It read:

> 11.35 am. Eng. 357 for 8
> McG. ct H-son b. Thos.   67
> Wms. not out   – 83
> O'B. not out   5

Mr Wilkins glanced at his watch. So the bulletin had been compiled less than twenty minutes before! Intrigued, he set about solving the mystery without betraying that he had discovered the plot.

Casually, he made his way round the room seeking further clues. On Martin-Jones' desk he found a hastily screwed-up slip of paper containing the information that England were 364 runs for eight wickets at 11.40 am. Farther along the row he picked up a crumpled pellet from the floor which told him that by 11.45 am the score had crept up to 372 without further loss of wickets.

Satisfied, Mr Wilkins continued on his way, tracking the information to its source. Soon he arrived at Jennings' desk at the end of the back row, where the occupant was bent low over his work, his head averted and his hand cupped over his left ear.

There Mr Wilkins stopped. Half a minute ticked by in a strained, unnatural silence while Form Three sat tense and aware, waiting for the blow to fall.

At last Mr Wilkins said, "I didn't know you were deaf, Jennings."

Jennings jumped slightly. "Me, sir? Oh no, sir, I'm not deaf, sir. I can hear ever so well."

"Then why do you wear a hearing-aid?" Gently, Mr Wilkins brushed aside the hand cupped to the ear and removed the earphone. He gave a slight tug, and the radio set shot out of Jennings' shirt pocket on the end of its lead.

"So that's the game, is it!" the master exclaimed in the tones of one who had unmasked the most diabolical plot of the century. "How dare you sit there listening to the radio in the middle of my lesson!"

There was nothing that Jennings could say in defence. Awkwardly, he mumbled, "Sorry, sir. I – er – I just wanted to know how the Test Match was going, before it was all over."

"Disgraceful behaviour! I never heard of such a thing!" Mr Wilkins swept his arm out in a gesture which included the whole class. "You're all involved in this. All of you! Passing bits of paper behind my back! I shall have this class in for detention later today for wilful and deliberate disobedience."

He strode to the master's desk and sat down with the miniature radio on the desk-top before him. "I shall confiscate this – this obnoxious little gadget, Jennings, and it's no use your asking for it back, because I've no intention of returning it before the end of the term."

Jennings' feelings turned to near-panic at the thought of having to tell the unsuspecting owner what had happened when he returned from the sick-room. What on earth would Bromo say! He'd go mad! There had been no detailed agreement about Jennings borrowing the set – merely a vague half-promise of a loan at some unspecified time in the future. And Bromwich would never have agreed to such an arrangement if he'd known that there would be the slightest risk of his property being impounded . . . Perhaps Mr Wilkins would relent when he knew the facts!

Jennings raised his hand and said, "Sir, please, sir, would you very kindly agree to let me have it back, if I tell you—"

"Of course you can't have it back! I'm surprised at your audacity in asking."

"Oh, but, sir, you don't understand. I don't mind having a different sort of punishment, but this is a special case, you see, because it doesn't belong—"

"Silence!" Mr Wilkins thundered. "One more word from you, Jennings, and I'll – I'll –" He searched his mind for a spine-chilling threat. Somewhat lamely, he finished up, "Well, there'd better not *be* one more word, that's all!"

All was quiet in Form Three classroom. The boys, subdued by the failure of the Test Match plan, worked at their problems in silence while Mr Wilkins sat scowling over the tops of their heads.

Then, a faint crackling sound on the desk-top caught the master's ear, and he realized that the radio set was still switched on. Abstractedly, he picked it up and held the earphone to his ear.

The ball-by-ball description was still on the air and, judging by the commentator's excited tones, the match was fast approaching its climax. England's last two batsmen were at the wicket, facing a determined West Indian attack. By now, only fifteen runs were needed for victory: could the tail-enders stay together long enough to save the game?

Mr Wilkins was a keen cricketer and a devoted follower of England's fortunes in the Test Match series. If he had not been teaching that morning, he would certainly have been listening to the commentary on the radio in his sitting-room. In a matter of minutes the match would be over: and as the boys were all hard at work, there seemed no reason why he shouldn't follow the game to its exciting close . . . Mr Wilkins slipped the earpiece comfortably into place and sat back to listen to the programme.

Martin-Jones was the first to finish the written work. He looked up and saw what Mr Wilkins was doing, and was shocked. To his way of thinking, it was natural enough that he and his friends should try to flout the rules, but surely a master ought to know better – especially after his recent outburst! Yet here was Old Wilkie calmly doing the same thing without batting an eyelid. It was scandalous!

Martin-Jones nudged his neighbour and pointed to the master's desk. The nudge travelled along the row and round the room until the whole class were staring at Mr Wilkins with unbelieving eyes.

Greatly daring, Venables asked, "Please, sir, what's the score?"

With an effort, Mr Wilkins forced his mind away from the scene of mounting excitement at the Old Trafford cricket ground. For a moment he bridled indignantly at the insolence of Venables' question. Then, meeting the gaze of all those pairs of eyes looking at him with every emotion from envy to astonishment, he realized how neatly he had turned the tables on the class. Their little scheme had backfired so completely that he was able to enjoy the fruits of the plan which they had plotted at his expense.

His anger evaporated and he smiled to himself.

He'd got them where he wanted them, and he decided to make the most of it!

Playing up to their curiosity, he let out a gasp of suspense and cried, "No! Oh no, surely not!"

The class jerked forward in their seats. "What happened, sir? . . . Is somebody out? . . . Is it all over?"

With an exaggerated gesture of caution, Mr Wilkins waved at them to be silent and pressed the earphone more firmly into place. For the next five minutes he played out the comedy, his face registering hope, despair, excitement and incredulity accompanied by sudden bursts of exclamation. "Oh, my goodness! He'll never do it! . . . Yes, he will! . . . No, he won't! . . . Phew! That was a near one!"

Form Three could hardly contain themselves. "But what's *happening*, sir? . . . Please tell us, sir . . . It's not fair!"

When the pantomime had run its course, Mr Wilkins removed the earphone and announced briskly, "Right! That's that, then. The match is over, so we can get on with our work."

"But who won, sir?" pleaded Rumbelow. "Won't you even tell us that?"

Mr Wilkins silenced him with a glance. "Are you out of your mind, Rumbelow?" he said. "Allow me to point out that we are in the middle of a maths lesson. We can't afford to waste valuable time talking about cricket."

The class exchanged baffled looks. "But that means we shall have to wait till we see it on telly this evening before we know what happened, sir," said Temple.

"See it on television! You must be joking!" Mr Wilkins retorted, pressing home his advantage. "I've already said that I shall be detaining this class for an hour, later on today. Very well, then! In order to make the punishment fit the crime, you boys will report here for an hour's detention after tea, instead of going to the library to watch television."

As the significance of the punishment struck home, the class closed ranks against the author of their misfortune.

"*Jennings*!" they jeered in derision. "It's all Jennings' fault. Trust him to get the whole class into a row!"

The culprit's gloom deepened. It was all very well for *them* to get steamed up about it, he reflected bitterly, but what about *him*! Missing an evening's telly was nothing compared to what *he'd* have to go through when old Bromo came down from the sick-room!

Chapter 6

Thunder in the Air

"It's no good going on worrying about what old Bromo's going to say," Darbishire told Jennings after cricket on Wednesday afternoon. "For all you know he may be suffering from bubonic plague or the Black Death or something: in which case he won't be down from the sick-room for ages – not until the end of term, perhaps."

Jennings refused to be comforted by the prospect of a long-drawn-out illness.

"How do you know he's got the Black Death? More likely, it's only an ingrowing chilblain. I bet you what you like, he'll come prancing back into school in a day or so and start beefing because he can't find his radio."

Darbishire grinned. "You'd better send him a greetings card saying, '*Don't* get well soon!' Anyway, we've got other things to think about – Sunday afternoon for instance."

For the time being they had had to postpone all thoughts of camp cookery because the fuel problem was still not resolved. Robinson seemed unwilling or unable to provide them with paraffin and the boys had

had no chance of obtaining supplies elsewhere. That being so, there was really no point in badgering Mrs Hackett for provisions which they would be unable to cook. However, as Darbishire pointed out, there were other things to be done in the meantime.

"I'm going to paint the walls just like those pictures of the Lascaux caves that Mr Hind showed us," he went on, as the boys made their way indoors from the cricket field to get ready for swimming. "I'd thought of doing spaceships and rockets taking off for Mars: but then I had another think and I thought that, as it's an ancient sort of cave, I'd do bisons and pterodactyls instead. More prehistorical, if you see what I mean."

Jennings wasn't particularly interested in Darbishire's views on interior decoration. "OK, you do as you like. I shall be busy with my pot-holing," he said. "I'm going to crawl along that passage and see how far it goes."

"What! In your best suit! You must be off your trolley. Mr Carter will blow his top if you come back all plastered with chalk. You heard what he said last Sunday."

Darbishire had raised a point of some importance. Head-room in the tunnel was obviously low. Any attempt to explore it on hands and knees would leave tell-tale marks on the clothing which might be impossible to remove at short notice. Such lack of foresight would not only lead to the discovery of their secret project, but might also result in the headmaster banning Sunday afternoon excursions for the whole school.

By this time the boys had reached the changing-room and were hurriedly getting into their swimming trunks. The school's indoor pool had been in use since the middle of May, and the half-hour after cricket practice was reserved on weekdays for the daily swim. On Sundays, swimming normally took place in the morning after letter-writing; but, whatever the time of day, the boys had learned not to waste precious minutes in the changing-room. The visit to the pool was yet another activity to be fitted into an already full programme of school routine, and five minutes squandered in getting ready meant five minutes less in the water.

Darbishire finished changing, grabbed his towel from his peg and rushed to join the throng streaming out of the room on their way to the pool. At the door he turned to see Jennings staring into space, his face puckered with concentration.

"Come on, Jen, for goodness sake! It won't be worth getting your trunks wet if you don't get a move on," he called, impatiently. "Mr Hind's taking swimming today, and he always blows the whistle early."

Jennings came out of his trance, picked up his towel and joined his friend in the doorway. He was chuckling with secret glee all the way along the corridor, across the playground and in through the double doors of the swimming pool.

"What's the big joke?" Darbishire asked.

"Aha!" said Jennings.

"Aha – what?"

"I've solved my pot-holing problem. I've just thought how to come back on Sunday looking all clean and tidy."

"If you're thinking of just taking a clothes brush with you, you're wasting your time. You wouldn't have a hope of getting all that chalk off before—"

"Who's talking about a clothes brush!" Jennings'

63

tone was scornful. "What I'm going to do is to put my swimming trunks on under my trousers before we give our names in to go out," he explained, as they stood together on the matting beside the pool. "So when we get there, I've only got to strip off and I shall be all ready for action in my pot-holing kit. Not a bad brainwave, eh!"

Darbishire beamed his congratulations. He was about to comment, but at that moment Mr Hind blew a long blast on the starting whistle and Jennings leapt into the water with a splash that soaked the duty master's trousers as he stood on the edge of the pool.

Most of the swimmers followed hard behind him, but Darbishire, a poor performer in the water, was never one to plunge in with a splash. Still smiling at the brilliant simplicity of his friend's brainwave, he pattered along the matting to the shallow end where, after testing the temperature with his toe, he lowered himself gingerly into the water.

Trust old Jen to solve the problem, he reflected, as he set off across the pool with a floundering breast-stroke. Everything was going to be all right, after all!

Shortly after lunch on Sunday, artist and pot-holer gave their names to Mr Wilkins and set off on their expedition.

Darbishire's trouser pockets bulged with little bottles of liquid poster paint – green, brown, red, yellow and blue; a selection of paint brushes was tucked out of sight down his socks. He was obliged to walk with extreme care until he was away from the school buildings as the containers rattled and clinked whenever he hurried his pace.

Jennings' equipment was even more uncomfortable. The bathing trunks which he was wearing under his trousers were still wringing wet from the morning swim and clung to him as a chilly reminder of the task that lay ahead. In addition to his torch, he was carrying his plimsolls tucked inside his shirt so that his outdoor shoes would bear no trace of his activities upon his return.

The afternoon was sultry with a hint of thunder in the air. Indeed, it was so warm that by the time the boys reached the cave and Jennings had stripped off his outer clothing, his swimming trunks were steaming in the heat. He made an untidy bundle of his clothes and put them down on the grass outside the entrance.

"I suppose I ought to be wearing a crash helmet," he remarked, pulling on his plimsolls. "I thought of borrowing Temple's astronaut's helmet, but it's only made of plastic, so it wouldn't be much use if the roof fell in."

Darbishire looked at him in sudden concern. "If the roof fell in!" he echoed. "It's not going to be dangerous, is it?"

"My little joke," Jennings explained. "Anyway, I'll be careful. Wish me luck, Darbi! If I find a hoard of hidden treasure, I'll buy you a brand new tennis racket."

Switching on his torch, he crossed the floor of the cave to the passage in the far wall. Then, on hands and knees, he crawled into the opening and disappeared from view.

Darbishire tried to follow his progress, but could see nothing except the rear view of the crouching pot-holer as he followed his torch beam into the darkness.

Shortly afterwards, Jennings' voice came echoing

back, amplified by the narrow confines of the tunnel.

"It's going to be a slow job, Darbi. There's fifty million tons of old boulders and loose chalk and stuff blocking the way along here. I'll have to shift it a handful at a time before I can get much farther."

In the outer cave the spongy texture of the walls and roof turned out to be a more difficult surface to work on than Darbishire had foreseen. The chalk soaked up the paint like blotting paper, and even after several applications the colours had a dull and faded look. But this was all to the good, the artist decided, for it created an impression of great age – which was much better than having to wait for the process to be carried out by time and weather!

So he persevered with his work, pausing only to shout reports of his progress to his unseen companion toiling away in the tunnel.

"I've done a Stone Age man chasing a brontosaurus across a swamp with a spear," he bawled down the opening after ten minutes' work. "I was going to do a squadron of pterodactyls overhead as well, but I couldn't remember which way their ears went. How are you getting on?"

Jennings answered with a grunt. He was far too absorbed in his task to worry about which way the ears of an extinct flying reptile should be pointing – or, indeed, to bother about whether it should have any ears at all!

On the roof, Darbishire painted a duck-billed platypus and a shaggy mammoth charging a Stone Age hunter whom he decided was the living image of Mr Wilkins. When he had finished he inspected his handiwork from all angles, and then went outside and peered in to see

how it would strike some future archaeologist redis-
covering the cave five thousand years hence.

It looked most realistic, he thought: a splendid
example of prehistoric cave art. If anything, it looked
even better when he took his glasses off, the slightly
blurred edges of the paintings suggesting exposure to
the weather and the ravages of time.

At that moment there was a rumble of thunder over
the Downs. The sun had already disappeared, and in
the distance black clouds were gathering for a summer
storm.

Darbishire looked at the weather and then glanced
down at Jennings' clothes lying where he had left them
on the grass slope beyond the entrance. They'd be soaked
in a matter of moments if the storm should happen to
break overhead. He put his glasses down on a ledge of
chalk, picked up the bundle and carried it inside.

They'd be safe enough under cover, he thought,
but how was he to keep them clean? The floor of
the cave was littered with loose chippings of chalk,
but in one corner was a narrow recess in the wall
formed by a natural cleft in the soft rock. A useful
cubby-hole, Darbishire decided, and just the place for
stowing articles tidily out of the way until they were
needed!

He pushed the bundle of clothes into the aperture
and then went out, intending to retrieve his glasses and
have another look at the weather. The storm seemed
to be holding off, but in any case they'd have to start
thinking of going back quite soon. He'd no idea how
long they'd been there; he'd been much too busy to
bother about time.

Darbishire peered at his watch. At once, his jaw

dropped and he gasped in dismay. Mindless of his spectacles, he rushed back into the cave and squawked down the tunnel.

"Hey, Jennings, quick! D'you know what the time is? Come on, for goodness sake, we've only got quarter of an hour to get back to school!"

The message whistled through the darkness and caught Jennings' ear as he came within an arm's length of the blank chalk wall marking the end of the tunnel.

It had taken him a long time to get so far. He had cleared away the debris and crawled along a passage some twenty yards in length, which sloped slightly downhill for most of the way and then dropped abruptly into a shallow pit about four feet deep. Here, for the first time, there was enough headroom to allow him to stand upright; but after that his torch beam showed nothing before him but a solid barrier of chalk.

He couldn't help feeling disappointed. He hadn't been expecting to find anything sensational: any reference to smugglers' hoards and pirates' treasure had been the sort of weak joke that anybody might have made in the circumstances.

All the same, he had hoped to find *something* – even a broken bedstead or a rusty bicycle wheel would have counted as a discovery of sorts, but now he had reached the end of the trail and there was nothing there at all.

Standing in the little pit, he cocked his head to hear what Darbishire was shouting about.

"OK, I'm coming now," he called back. "We'll get going as soon as I've got my things on."

"But there isn't *time*! Even if we run all the way we'll still be late. They're bound to ask questions and find out where we've been."

This was true enough. Not only would their own plans be thwarted, but they would be held responsible for the whole school losing the privilege of unsupervised walks on Sunday afternoons.

"What on earth are we going to *do*?" Darbishire's voice, amplified by the tunnel, was shrill with panic.

Jennings thought fast. "You go on ahead and report that you're back. I'll come as soon as I'm dressed."

"But we've *both* got to report, if we went out together. Supposing Old Wilkie asks where you are?"

"Tell him you'll go and find me. That'll waste a few minutes, and with any luck I ought to be back by then."

"Yes, but what if—?"

"Oh, go *on*, Darbi," Jennings stormed. "There isn't a second to lose."

Darbishire scrambled out of the cave, slithered down the bank and tore through the jungle of gorse bushes in his desperate race against time.

The storm had passed without breaking, but the oppressive heat of the afternoon soon took its toll of the breathless runner. Darbishire was no athlete, and now his face was scarlet and his forehead streamed with perspiration; his shirt clung damply to his body and his socks were puckered about his ankles. Gasping for breath and wheezing with effort, he plodded on over downland and meadow and along the footpath past Arrowsmith's farm.

He was just turning in through the gate at the far end of the school grounds when he remembered that he had left his glasses lying outside the cave!

Jennings wasn't prepared for the disaster when it struck . . . He came wriggling back through the tunnel and into the daylight a few moments after Darbishire's departure. In frantic haste he rushed out of the cave to retrieve his clothes.

They were not there!

With mounting anxiety he looked round for some clue to their whereabouts. But the downward slope was bare of foliage; so, too, was the steeply rising hillside above the cave mouth. There wasn't so much as a gorse bush or a molehill to provide a shred of cover within twenty yards in any direction.

So where on earth could they be? He'd left them on a patch of level ground: they couldn't possibly have rolled all the way down to the little crater at the bottom. And even if they *had*, they would still have been in sight.

Had Darbishire hidden them for a joke? The theory didn't make sense. Darbishire wouldn't play a trick like that – well, not at a time like this, when the only thought in his head had been to get them both back to school in the shortest possible time. They couldn't have been stolen. There was nobody about: they hadn't seen a soul all afternoon!

Jennings was utterly bewildered. Unaware of the storm clouds which had prompted his friend's little act of kindness, he could find no solution to the baffling mystery which confronted him.

Panic seized the unfortunate pot-holer. He went back into the cave, certain that he would find nothing, but unable to think of anywhere else to look. A quick glance convinced him that the cave was empty. Darbishire's cubby-hole was in a dark corner, and the bundle had been pushed well back into the recess.

Jennings flipped his fingers in despair. He couldn't stay where he was, yet how could he go back to school in his swimming trunks without being spotted by any

master who happened to be strolling about the grounds!
Already he was overdue. When his absence was discovered, Darbishire would be questioned and the facts
would come to light. They'd send a search party to look
for him. Should he wait until they found him, or should
he report back to school in his bathing trunks?

Either way, he'd be in trouble! His only hope lay (as
Mr Hind might have observed) in choosing the lesser of
two evils.

He decided to return . . .

The journey back to school was a nightmare. As he
made his way through the thickets, briars tore at his
bare legs and blackberry brambles whipped against his
arms and chest. He was glad there was no one about to
observe his painful progress. The only living creature he
saw was Mr Arrowsmith's obstinate sheep which again
appeared to have strayed from the flock in search of
new pastures.

Things were a little better when he was clear of
the undergrowth and on the open downland. He ran
full speed till he reached the meadow and set off on
the last lap across the field path.

Mr Arrowsmith was leaning on a gate as the runner
passed by. "Bit warm for a cross-country run, isn't it,"
the farmer observed genially.

Jennings gave him a sickly smile and hurried past.

As he turned in through the bottom gate to the school
grounds, his heart was thumping and his mind was blank
with despair. In a matter of minutes he would be face
to face with an incredulous master demanding to know
the reason for his skimpy attire. There was no way out,
unless . . .!

He slackened his pace and forced his bemused brain

to take another look at the problem. If he approached the building from the rear, skirting the kitchen garden and avoiding the playground, he might be able to slip unobserved through the basement window of the tuck-box room. From there, if his luck still held, he could creep up the back stairs to the clothing lockers on the landing outside Dormitory Four and retrieve his everyday clothes.

He might have some awkward questions to answer when he reported to the master on duty, but at least he would be spared the blood-curdling embarrassment of walking into the staff-room wearing nothing but his ridiculous cotton bathing trunks.

Screening himself behind the bushes and darting from tree to tree, Jennings made his stealthy approach to the rear of the school buildings. So far as he could see there was nobody about on the playing-fields – which was surprising at that hour of the afternoon. However, it suited his purpose: the fewer spectators the better, at this tricky stage of the proceedings.

He reached the basement window, pushed up the sash and crawled through: the tuck-box room was empty. He tiptoed to the door and peered out, hope riding high now that he had come so far without being spotted.

His luck still held: there was nobody in sight. Once round the bend in the corridor, he would make a dash for the stairs, and from then onwards it should all be plain sailing.

But he'd have to be quick! There was nowhere to take cover now, so the sooner he was out of the danger area, the better. Darting out of the tuck-box room, he ran at full speed along the corridor . . .

As he rounded the corner, he collided head-on with the headmaster proceeding in the opposite direction!

Chapter 7

The Bogus Bug-Hunters

Mr Pemberton-Oakes, headmaster of Linbury Court School, was a quietly-spoken man who held progressive views about the upbringing of the younger generation. However, even the most enlightened of headmasters draws the line at being butted in the stomach by eleven-year-old boys in swimming trunks.

"Ouch!" exclaimed the headmaster, recoiling from the blow. "Why on earth don't you look where you're going, you clumsy little boy?"

For a moment, Jennings was too appalled by the disaster to do anything but hop from foot to foot in guilty confusion. The worst had happened: there was nothing he could say to justify his embarrassing choice of clothing.

At last he faltered, "I'm terribly sorry, sir. I didn't think you'd be there, sir – I mean, I was in a hurry, you see. I've just come back from a walk."

Even as he spoke, he realized it was the feeblest excuse he had ever been called upon to offer. People didn't *go* for Sunday afternoon walks in swimming trunks and plimsolls! He waited with apprehension for the searching questions to begin.

"Why on earth don't you look where you're going, you clumsy little boy?" exclaimed the headmaster.

Mr Pemberton-Oakes looked down at the squirming culprit and said, "What are you looking so agitated about, Jennings? Is there anything wrong?"

It wasn't the question Jennings had been expecting.

Was anything wrong! Couldn't the headmaster *see* what was wrong? With seventy-eight of his pupils properly dressed in school uniform, did it not occur to him to wonder why the seventy-ninth should be prancing round the passages dressed as a cherub!

Jennings gulped slightly and said, "No, sir. Nothing wrong, sir – at least, not really, sir."

"In that case you'd better run along and join the eager throng, before it's too late."

"Join the *who*, sir?"

"The rest of the school. They're waiting for you on the playground."

"Yes, sir."

Jennings was dumbfounded. Not a word about the swimming trunks! Had the headmaster taken leave of his eyesight? Had the strain of presiding over Linbury Court School for so many years unhinged his mind?

In a daze, Jennings turned and made his way along the corridor. With the headmaster standing in full view of the staircase, he would have to postpone his visit to the clothing lockers until the coast was clear. Still bemused, he continued as far as the side door and went out on to the playground, according to instructions.

There, as the headmaster had told him, the whole school were waiting – *all of them wearing swimming trunks* and carrying towels!

Venables spotted Jennings as he came through the door. "Hurry up, Jen, for goodness sake! Mr Wilkins won't let us in till everybody's ready."

"Won't let you in where?"

"The pool, of course. You don't imagine we're going for a swim in the long-jump pit, do you!"

Light dawned in Jennings' mind. So that was why the headmaster had accepted his appearance without question. "But we had swimming this morning. Why are we going in again now?" he queried.

"Why not? It's a hot day. Some of the blokes asked the Head when we got back from the walk, and he said we could have another swim."

Jennings felt weak at the knees with relief. Two visits to the swimming pool on a Sunday were unusual, but not unheard of. By a lucky chance he had picked about the only day in the term when his unorthodox dress in the corridor would pass unnoticed.

"You took long enough getting ready," Venables complained. "Sir threatened to cancel it if he had to wait much longer for the stragglers to turn up."

"Sorry! I didn't know about it till now. I've only just come back."

"You must have known, or you wouldn't have got changed," Venables pointed out.

Jennings pulled a face. "I got changed hours ago. Just on the off-chance, you know."

By now the boys were filing into the swimming pool and Jennings rushed ahead, hoping to catch up with Darbishire whom he had just seen disappearing into the building. Not for a moment did he suspect that his friend could have been the author of his misfortunes. His only concern was to report the mysterious facts and discuss what was to be done about them.

However, when he reached the entrance he was stopped by Mr Wilkins who sent him all the way back to the changing-room to fetch a towel. By the time he returned, the swimmers were in the water and he was obliged to postpone the conference with his friend about the loss of his best clothes.

Thus it was not until swimming was over and the boys had finished changing, that Jennings (now dressed in his everyday clothes) found a chance to take Darbishire aside for a few words in private behind the shoe-lockers.

"Listen, Darbi," be began. "Something terrible's happened."

"Yes, I know. I left my glasses behind at the cave. Did you bring them back?"

"Never mind your glasses! Wait till you hear what happened to me. When I came out of the tunnel, my clothes had gone."

Far from being shattered by the announcement, Darbishire merely said, "Yes, I know. I shifted them."

Jennings nearly had a heart attack. "*You did what*!"

"I moved them for you. I bunged them into a sort of little cubby-hole, just inside. Didn't you find them?"

"I should flipping well think I *didn't* find them," Jennings stormed. He was shocked, horrified, bewildered. "Honestly, Darbi, you must be off your trolley! What in the name of thunder did you go and do a crazy thing like that for?"

"I was only trying to be helpful," Darbishire defended himself. "I thought it was going to rain, you see, and so—"

"And so you hid my clothes where you knew I couldn't possibly find them, and then went laughing your stupid great head off all the way back to school, thinking how clever you'd been! Talk about treachery!

Talk about sabotage! I never thought any friend of mine would play a dirty trick like that."

"Oh no, honestly!" Darbishire was appalled by the accusation. "I didn't do it on purpose. I thought you'd be bound to find them when you came out."

"How could I find them if you'd hidden them? Why didn't you tell me what you'd done?"

The culprit bit his lip and mumbled, "Sorry, Jen, I forgot."

Jennings thumped the nearest shoe-locker in frustration. "*Forgot*! How could you forget a thing like that?"

"I was in a hurry," Darbishire explained unhappily. "I got a bit flustered when I saw how late it was. And you told me to go on ahead and – well, I didn't even remember my glasses, let alone your clothes."

Through the open window they could hear distant laughter and the friendly exchange of insults between Temple and Atkinson playing a riotous game of French cricket on the playing-field. Their voices seemed to belong to another world – a happy, carefree world untouched by the tragedy of losing one's vital possessions.

Darbishire shook his head sadly and said, "All the same, it was a pity you didn't think of bringing my glasses back. You must have noticed them. They were on that little ledge just outside—"

He broke off and dodged as Jennings hurled a plimsoll at him in exasperation. "You and your glasses! You and your stupid old glasses!" he shouted. "What about me and my best clothes! That's a thousand times worse, and it's all your fault."

"All right, you needn't go on about it. I was only going to say—"

"Well, don't say it! I don't want to hear it. I've finished with you and your dirty tricks, Darbishire! Finished with you for ever!".

So saying, Jennings turned and strode from the room, slamming the door behind him.

Mr Carter noticed that Darbishire wasn't wearing his glasses when he strolled round the dining-hall during tea. From the guarded – and somewhat garbled – reply that he received to his inquiry, he assumed that the owner had lost them somewhere within the school precincts.

"Did you leave them in the changing-room?" he asked.

Darbishire shook his head. On that point he was quite definite.

"And he wasn't wearing them when we went to swimming," Rumbelow put in from across the tea-table. "I can prove it, because I walked over to the pool with him."

"In that case we'd better organize a thorough search after tea," Mr Carter decided. "If we get the whole school on the job, somebody's sure to find them."

Darbishire shrank with embarrassment. "Oh, no, sir, don't do that," he pleaded. "It wouldn't be any good, anyway, because – because—"

He faltered to a stop. How could he explain that a search would be pointless without betraying the fact that he knew perfectly well where his wretched spectacles were! And that would lead to further questions and the collapse of their secret project. "I shouldn't want to put everybody to a lot of trouble," he finished up.

"Nonsense! This is a serious matter," the master replied. He called for silence in the dining-hall and made an announcement.

"Quiet, please! . . . Put your cup down, Venables, when I'm speaking."

"Sorry, sir."

"So I should think! Now, Darbishire has lost his glasses, so after tea we're all going to have to look for them. We'll split up into groups and go over the building and the playing-fields with a fine-tooth comb. The finder will be richly rewarded with – er – with the owner's undying gratitude."

Some of the boys had been hoping to play tennis or informal cricket after tea; others had planned to devote an hour to model-making or arranging their stamp albums. For this reason, Darbishire's popularity was at a low ebb when the search parties set out on their quest.

"Mouldy old Darbishire! Three boos for Darbi," complained Blotwell, who felt strongly about having to cancel his plans to clean out his caterpillars. "Why can't he look for them by himself?"

"He wouldn't be able to see them, that's why," his friend, Binns, pointed out. "If you're as short-sighted as Darbishire, you have to be wearing your glasses before you can start looking for them."

"Well, I don't see how we're going to be much help. We haven't got one of those fine-tooth combs that Mr Carter was talking about."

Needless to say, the search proved fruitless so far as Darbishire's spectacles were concerned. On the credit side, however, a number of long-lost articles came to light in various places, including thirteen assorted cricket and tennis balls, six ballpoint pens, four old plimsolls, a roller skate, a bicycle pump, Venables' telescope and Blotwell's pyjama trousers.

Wracked with guilt, Darbishire followed the searchers round the cricket field, pretending to hunt through the long grass in the outfield, for the sake of appearances. Behind the pavilion he met Jennings, still hostile from their recent quarrel.

"Now see what you've done!" Jennings greeted him in resentful tones. "Everybody's had to give up their free time just because of you. I shouldn't be surprised if you left your old specs behind on purpose, just to be awkward."

Coming from Jennings, of all people, the accusation seemed grossly unfair. Angrily, Darbishire protested, "You're a fine one to talk! If Mr Carter knew what had really happened this afternoon, you'd be in a spot of trouble too, don't forget!"

Jennings' resentment faded. "Perhaps you're right," he agreed. "Actually there *is* a funny side to it – the whole school poking about in the shrubbery and more or less getting floor-boards up, when you and I know they haven't a hope of finding them."

With a ludicrous gesture he knelt down and inspected the underside of a dock-leaf. "Famous detective searching for clues in the *Case of the Missing Spectacles*," he announced with mock importance. "According to my theory, Mr Darbishire, I'd say they've been stolen by an international gang of spectacle thieves in a daring daylight robbery."

"You needn't try to be funny. There could be a row about it, if Mr Carter found out," Darbishire said.

"Yes, I know." Jennings dropped his jocular tone. "That's why we've got to do something about it before it's too late. We must think of a plan."

"*We*?" The memory of the quarrel before tea flashed

into Darbishire's mind. "You and me together, d'you mean? You said you'd finished with me: you said we weren't going to be friends any more."

Jennings dismissed the hard feelings with a wave of his hand. "I'll let you off this time – give you another chance."

"Thanks! Very generous of you, I'm sure," Darbishire said coldly.

"Well, you know what I mean! We're both in the same spot of trouble, so we'll have to stick together."

As usual, the quarrel had been no more than the short-lived resentment caused by a frustrating set of circumstances. Darbishire was glad it was over. He said, "Righto, then, but what are we going to do?"

Jennings frowned in thought. His own plight was more serious than that of his friend. The loss of Darbishire's glasses might well be passed off as an unfortunate accident, but the disappearance of an almost new grey suit, complete with shirt, socks and shoes, would be impossible to explain. Every Monday morning, when the best clothes were put back in the lockers, Matron would run her eye over the garments for signs of wear and tear: the empty shelf in Jennings' locker was bound to lead to questions.

"One of us will have to fox back to the cave and fetch them," Jennings decided. "Toss up for it, shall we?"

Butterflies fluttered inside Darbishire's stomach. "What *now*! In broad daylight! We'd never get away with it," he quavered. "Somebody would see us. And, anyway, the dorm bell would have gone before we got back, and Mr Carter's on duty, don't forget."

The objection was valid. It would be futile to risk

leaving the premises without permission at a time when everybody's movements could be easily checked by the master on duty.

It wasn't often that Jennings was unable to think of some way of avoiding a crisis, but now he had to admit defeat. Gloomily, he said, "We'd better go and own up, then. There's nothing else we can do."

At that moment, Binns and Blotwell ambled round the corner of the pavilion, grumbling about the loss of their free time. Mindful, however, of Mr Carter's instructions, they were still half-heartedly going through the motions of searching for the missing glasses.

When they saw Jennings and Darbishire talking together in low tones, Binns nudged his companion and said loudly, "Hey! How about that, then! Here's us doing old Darbishire's dirty work for him while he's skulking behind the pav, not bothering to help."

"Hear hear! Flipping well not fair! Loud boos and hisses," his friend agreed.

Had things been otherwise, lowly juniors such as Binns and Blotwell might have thought twice before so outspokenly criticizing a third-former within earshot. But now that nobody had any sympathy left for Darbishire and his problem, the youngest boys in the school felt able to speak their minds without fear of reprisals.

"Buzz off, Binns. We don't want any cheek from Form One," Jennings said curtly.

"No, but honestly!" the first-former protested. "Darbishire's gone and mucked up our whole evening. Thanks to him, we've got to get up early tomorrow and do our caterpillars before breakfast."

"So what! It won't hurt you to . . ." Jennings paused and his face creased in a wide smile. An idea had just occurred to him! "Well, since you've been so kind in helping old Darbi to look for his specs, we'll both get up early and help you, won't we, Darbi!"

"Me? I never said I'd do anything of the—"

"Don't argue, Darbi. It won't hurt you to stroll round, picking a few handfuls of leaves, will it!"

Binns frowned with suspicion. "Is this a trick, or are you just taking the mickey?" he demanded.

"Neither. We want to help," Jennings assured him. "You carry on looking for his glasses, and we'll join your bug-hunting expedition before breakfast."

When the two younger boys had departed, Jennings outlined the purpose of his plan. Hunting for caterpillars and collecting fresh leaves for their food, provided a ready-made excuse for boys to wander at will all over the school grounds in the early hours of the morning.

Under cover of a genuine expedition, he explained, they would set out soon after the rising bell, taking with them the usual paper bags and cardboard boxes for the storage of specimens. As they went, they would pick a few leaves to camouflage their activities. Then, when they had made their way as far as the bottom gate, Jennings would slip through unobserved and hurry off to the cave, while Darbishire remained on guard at the gate to check that the coast was clear for his return.

"It's foolproof. There's nothing to go wrong," Jennings finished up. "I'll be back before the breakfast bell, and we can troop indoors with Binns and Blotwell and Co all carrying our little bags and boxes – the only difference being that *our* boxes will be full of my best clothes instead of caterpillar leaves."

"And my glasses," Darbishire reminded him.

"You won't want a shoebox for your glasses. They'll

be on your nose by that time." Jennings grinned. "You should be really popular at breakfast, because everybody will know they can stop looking."

Unlike most of Jennings' schemes, the *Plan of the Bogus Bug-Hunters*, as he insisted upon calling it, worked smoothly and gave little cause for alarm.

Setting off in company with a group of genuine caterpillar-fanciers, Jennings and Darbishire soon wandered away from Binns and Blotwell and the others and hurried off to the bottom gate to put Jennings' plan into operation.

The next half hour was something of a strain for Darbishire. He had explained to Jennings in great detail the exact whereabouts of the articles to be recovered, and had drawn sketch-maps with X marking the cubbyhole in the cave and Y marking the chalk ledge outside the entrance.

Provided that Jennings didn't actually break his leg, get chased by a bull, eat poisonous toadstools or trip over an unexploded bomb, there was really no reason to prevent his returning on schedule, bearing the salvaged possessions in triumph . . . Even so, Darbishire was tense and anxious during the time of waiting.

Shortly after Jennings' departure, Binns and Blotwell passed by on their quest for puss-moth eggs.

"What are you doing down here, Darbi?" Blotwell asked, stopping by the gate. "You won't find much stuff around these parts. The best trees are over by the pond."

"I'm all right where I am," the bogus bug-hunter said, warily. "Actually, I'm only collecting leaves. I can't see caterpillars properly without my glasses."

"You should eat more carrots, then you wouldn't

need glasses," said Binns. "Carrots are ever so good for the eyesight. Donkeys eat them by the hundredweight: that's why they can see so well."

"I'm not a donkey and I don't like carrots," the guard at the gate said coldly. "And, anyway, how d'you know they've got good eyesight?"

Binns wrinkled his nose and said, "Stands to reason! You don't often see a donkey wearing glasses, do you!"

Blotwell hooted with laughter at what he seemed to think was a sparkling gem of humour, but Darbishire merely snorted and said, "Buzz off, both of you. I've got more important things to do than stand around listening to feeble Form One jokes."

Chapter 8

Doubtful Security

At ten minutes to eight, Mr Wilkins' whistle summoned the naturalists indoors to get ready for breakfast. They straggled past him in ones and twos, some of them stopping to thrust a battered shoebox under the master's nose with an invitation to inspect the newly acquired specimens crawling about inside.

Jennings and Darbishire, however, extended no such invitation; for the very good reason that their cardboard containers were crammed to the lids with various articles of clothing and a pair of shoes.

Mr Wilkins didn't appear to notice that Darbishire was wearing his spectacles when he walked past him. At any rate he made no reference to the fact, merely telling the boy to go and wash his hands before breakfast.

"Did you see anyone?" Darbishire asked, when Mr Wilkins was safely out of earshot.

"Only Arrowsmith's old sheep, mooching about miles from the others," Jennings replied. "I always seem to run into her, every time I go anywhere near the camp site."

Once inside the building, Jennings rushed upstairs to replace the salvaged garments in his locker. He was only just in time, for Matron was already at work supervising the return of the best clothes. When he went downstairs again, he found Darbishire waiting for him in the hall. To Jennings' surprise, his friend was *not* wearing his glasses.

"I've hidden them," Darbishire explained in answer to Jennings' query. "I suddenly got the wind up when I walked past Old Wilkie just now. Luckily, he didn't spot them, but supposing he *had*! He'd have asked me where I found them and I should have had to say, well . . . " Darbishire was essentially a truthful boy: he didn't mind trailing a red herring to confuse Mr Wilkins, but he couldn't bring himself to tell a lie about it. "Well, it would have given the game away, wouldn't it!"

"Yes, I expect so, but what's the point of my getting them back for you, if you're going to lose them again?" Jennings demanded.

Darbishire smiled. "So that *someone else* can find them. Rather crafty, really! Whoever finds them now will think they've been there all the time," he explained. "And that means I shan't have to answer any awkward questions."

It wasn't long before Darbishire's trap was sprung . . . Shortly before morning school, Mr Wilkins was standing outside the assembly hall when Rumbelow approached at a fast trot.

"Sir! Sir! What do you think, sir! Famous discovery! I've just found Darbishire's glasses in the washroom," he announced, waving the delicate objects round his head by one earpiece.

"Good!" Mr Wilkins removed the spectacles before Rumbelow's impersonation of an Olympic hammer-thrower had resulted in permanent damage. "Send Darbishire to me, will you!"

Darbishire, summoned from the common-room, greeted the return of his property with a spate of thanks and a look of wide-eyed innocence.

"Oh, thank you, sir. Thank you very much indeed. I was quite lost without them," he said, polishing the glasses on the sleeve of his sweater.

"They were in the washroom," Rumbelow informed him. "But what I can't understand is that I searched all along that shelf yesterday evening, and I never spotted them. I'm sure they weren't there then."

"They weren't there first thing this morning, either," said Martin-Jones who was loitering within earshot. "I know, because I went all round the washroom collecting the dirty towels for Matron. I couldn't have helped seeing them, if they'd been there."

"Really!" Something stirred in Mr Wilkins' memory. In his mind's eye there flashed a clear picture of Darbishire walking past him with his spectacles on his nose as he returned from his caterpillar hunt before breakfast. Puzzled, he said, "Did *you* put them in the washroom this morning, Darbishire?"

The culprit blushed scarlet in guilt and confusion. His little ruse had collapsed. Awkwardly, he mumbled, "Yes, sir."

"In heaven's name, why?"

Darbishire's confusion grew. "I wanted somebody else to find them," he faltered. "Everybody went to an awful lot of trouble looking for them, you see, so I thought it wouldn't really be fair to all the other blokes, if I found them myself."

Fortunately, it didn't occur to Mr Wilkins to inquire *where* Darbishire had found his property. He merely heaved a sigh of exasperation and said, "Tut – tut –

tut! You really *are* a silly little boy, Darbishire!"

"Yes, sir. I know, sir," Darbishire agreed.

The bell rang for morning assembly and the duty master strode off to the staff-room to collect some books for the first lesson. In the corridor he met Mr Carter on his way to the assembly hall.

"Honestly, Carter, some of these boys get the most fantastic ideas. I just don't understand the way their so-called minds appear to work," he complained in tones of baffled incredulity. "Take Darbishire, for instance – he's got his glasses back now, by the way."

"I'm delighted to hear it," said Mr Carter.

"Yes, but that isn't all. Having found them once, the silly little boy goes and hides them again in case anybody thinks he hadn't lost them properly the first time. I ask you, does that make sense?"

Mr Carter smiled. "It sounds a little odd," he agreed, "but knowing Darbishire, I'd say he had his reasons!"

Bromwich came back into school at break that morning, glowing with health. The first thing he did upon leaving the sick-room was to go to his locker in the common-room to look for his miniature radio.

A cry of puzzled protest rang out as he ran his eye over the shelves. "Hey! What's been going on? My set's been stolen!"

Atkinson looked up from the table where he was arranging his stamp collection. "Don't panic! It's only been borrowed," he explained.

"Borrowed! Who said anybody could borrow it! *I* never did!"

Atkinson shrugged. He could foresee trouble ahead

when the owner found out what had happened, and he had no wish to get involved in the argument. "Better ask Jennings," he advised. "He knows all about it."

Bromwich ran Jennings to earth in the tuck-box room where, in Darbishire's company, he was fortifying himself with a fruit cake he had just received in a parcel from home.

"Hey, Jennings, I want a word with you," he began angrily.

It was obvious to the cake-eaters what subject the new arrival had come to discuss. Jennings gave him a disarming smile and said, "Ah, hallo, Bromo! Glad to see you're better. Would you like a piece of cake?"

"No!" barked Bromwich.

Darbishire was shocked by this breach of good manners. "No – *what*?" he prompted.

"No *fear*," said Bromwich. "You can keep your mouldy old cake. I want to know who gave you permission to borrow my radio."

"You did," said Jennings.

"Me!" Bromwich was nonplussed. "I never did anything of the sort . . . When?"

"About three weeks ago. Don't you remember? I was looking after it while I was umpiring, and you said I could borrow it some time when you weren't using it."

Bromwich cast his mind back to the day in question. Frowning, he muttered, "Ah yes, but I didn't mean you could take it without telling me."

"I couldn't tell you, could I! You were in the sick-room," Jennings pointed out. "And you certainly weren't using it, because you hadn't taken it with you."

"Yes, I dare say, but that doesn't give you the right to—" Bromwich broke off, unwilling to pursue an argument that he felt was getting him nowhere. "All right, then, but you should have put it back again afterwards." He thrust out his hand in a peremptory gesture. "I'll have it back now, please. Hand it over!"

Darbishire looked out of the window and said, "No point in beating about the bush. You'd better tell him, Jen."

Jennings' disarming smile wavered a little at the edges.

"Well, a rather unfortunate thing has happened, Bromo," he began, hoping to break the news gently. "You see, we were using your set to listen to the Test Match, and quite by chance, as it were – er – purely by accident, as you might say – or rather, by the merest stroke of bad luck—"

"Are you trying to tell me you've bust it?" Bromwich broke in furiously. "Because if you have, I'll – I'll – I'll—" He spluttered to a halt, unable to think of any torture horrifying enough to avenge such an act of villainy.

"Oh no, it's quite safe," Jennings assured him. "Safer, actually, than it was in your locker, because Mr Wilkins is very kindly looking after it for you. The only snag is," he finished up uncertainly, "the only real problem is that he refuses to give it back."

Bromwich's temper was not improved when he learned about the confiscation. Neither was he consoled by Jennings' offer to go and see Mr Wilkins again and make another plea for the return of the impounded property.

"He won't give it back – I know Old Wilkie," he declared, scowling at the shoe-lockers and blowing out his cheeks in protest. "It flipping well isn't fair."

"Perhaps if we were to chat him up and be specially nice to him for a few days," suggested Darbishire. "You know, extra polite and all that sort of flannel. It might soften him up."

"Huh! You'd need a bulldozer to soften up Sir," Bromwich snorted. He rounded angrily on Jennings. "It's all very well for you. It's not your set. But how do I know he'll *ever* give it back!"

"Of course he will. He said he'd give it back at the end of term."

"*Which* term? This term, next term, some term, never term? That's no use to me! I want it a whole lot sooner than that."

A number of boys had drifted into the tuck-box room while the argument was going on. All agreed that Bromwich had a genuine grievance and that it was up to Jennings to do something about it.

"I reckon he ought to give Bromo some sort of security," Venables suggested.

"Security?" echoed Rumbelow. "Police dogs and armoured cars, and things?"

"Not *that* sort of security. I mean something valuable of his own for Bromo to hang on to until he gets his radio back," Venables explained. "It's like, say, for instance, if someone borrows a thousand pounds from the bank, they have to hand over the deeds of their house in case they don't pay it back."

"But Jennings hasn't *got* a house, so how could he hand over the deeds?" Rumbelow persisted.

"That's just an *example*, you clodpoll," Venables said impatiently. "The point is that if Bromo has got something belonging to Jennings, Jennings will try all the harder to get round Old Wilkie: otherwise, he'll never get his security back."

Everybody agreed that the solution was a fair one; everybody looked at Jennings to see what sort of security he was prepared to offer.

For a moment Jennings stood frowning in thought. Then he turned and rummaged through the untidy contents of his tuck-box and brought out the dingy oil painting formerly described in the Dunhambury Auction Mart catalogue as *Country Scene in Spring – Artist unknown – 15in x 8in*.

"How about this, then! A genuine old master," he announced proudly, holding the picture up for inspection. "It's worth a hundred times more than Bromo's radio set."

With the exception of Atkinson and Darbishire, nobody in the group had seen the picture before, and now that they had a chance to examine it, they didn't seem to think highly of it as a work of art.

"I'm not taking *that* as security," Bromwich protested in disgust. "Dirty, faded, tatty old thing! You can hardly make out what it's meant to be."

"That's because it's so ancient: that's what proves it's priceless," Jennings maintained.

"Huh! I bet!"

"I can prove it!" Jennings voice throbbed with conviction. "Go to the National Gallery! Go to the Tate Gallery! Go to the Louvre! All the most famous, priceless old paintings look as though they've been left out in the rain since the Middle Ages."

"Well, if it's so priceless, what's it doing in your tuck-box?" Venables demanded.

In a few words, Jennings told them how the picture

had come into his possession, calling upon Atkinson (a willing witness) to confirm the truth of his story.

". . . and then this old lady came up and told me not to part with it on any account," he went on, noting with interest that his audience were listening in spellbound fascination. "She said it might be worth thousands of pounds, some day. She knew what she was talking about, all right! I could tell she was an Art expert because she was wearing a special, artistic sort of hat." He turned to Bromwich with a reassuring smile. "You couldn't ask for a better security than a valuable old master worth thousands of pounds, could you!"

A few members of the group were inclined to believe him; others were sceptical, but lacked the expert knowledge with which to disprove Jennings' extravagant claims.

Finally, Bromwich said grudgingly, "Well, all right then. I suppose I'll have to take it if it's the best you can do, but I'd rather have my radio than this grotty old painting, any day. And if I don't get it back soon," he went on in menacing tones, "there's going to be some bashing-up going on around these parts, so you'd better get cracking, Jennings – or else!"

The bell rang for the end of break and the boys dispersed to their classrooms, still arguing about the authenticity of Jennings' priceless old master.

Mr Wilkins was marking books in the staff-room shortly after lunch when Mr Carter came into the room and made an entry on the engagement pad pinned to the noticeboard.

"Slight change of programme," he announced. "I've just been talking to the Head, and he thinks we ought

95

to take advantage of this fine weather and arrange a picnic for the school on Wednesday. It'll mean missing the last two periods on Wednesday morning, but I don't suppose the boys will complain about that!"

"Neither shall I," said Mr Wilkins. "I'd agree to a picnic in a crocodile swamp, if it meant a break from teaching Form Three for a couple of lessons."

Mr Carter laughed. "It needn't be a crocodile swamp – unless you *insist*! I thought we'd take them to that spot on the Downs where we went last year. It's just about the right distance, and there's that great jungle of gorse bushes for them to explore during the afternoon."

Briefly, Mr Carter outlined the arrangements he had in mind. He and Mr Hind would set out on foot with the main body of the school at morning break, following the footpath past Arrowsmith's farm which led up to the Downs. As the headmaster would not be coming, Mr Wilkins was to be in charge of transporting the food and other provisions in the school mini-bus. This would mean his taking a different route from the walkers, as the downland paths were unsuitable for vehicles. However, by making a detour and following a farm track, he would be able to drive the bus to a point not far from the rendezvous which Mr Carter had decided upon.

"Don't try to take the van over the top or you'll be in trouble," Mr Carter advised. "If I were you, I'd take a few volunteers to hump the baskets and things along to the picnic spot."

"Fair enough," Mr Wilkins agreed. "And I'll pick my volunteers with some care. I don't want to find that half the food has mysteriously disappeared on the journey."

As they were talking, there came a knock on the door

and Jennings sidled into the room, looking more than usually subdued for one of his lively temperament.

"Sir, please, sir, Mr Wilkins, sir, may I speak to you?" he inquired in diffident tones.

"Speak on!" Mr Wilkins commanded.

"Well, sir, I was wondering whether you'd very kindly let me have that radio back that you confiscated in class last week."

"Certainly not! I'm surprised at your asking," the master said severely. "Boys who deliberately misuse their property during my lesson deserve to be deprived of it."

"But it isn't *my* property, sir. It belongs to Bromwich. I'd only borrowed it."

Mr Wilkins shrugged. "That'll teach him to be more careful whom he lends it to in future."

Jennings shuffled his feet in confusion. "Yes, I know, sir, only – well, he didn't even *know* that I'd borrowed it. And now he's come down from the sick-room and found out, he's kicking up a – I mean, he's not very pleased about it, if you see what I mean."

"I'm sure he isn't," Mr Wilkins agreed. "Naturally, he holds you to blame, but that's no reason why you should expect me to come to your rescue and save you from Bromwich's wrath and indignation."

"No, sir. Only, I thought that if you'd give me a different sort of punishment instead, I should be quite willing to—"

"It's no good arguing, Jennings. If Bromwich is out for your blood, that's *your* problem – not mine. You should have thought of the consequences before you disrupted my lesson: it's too late now." Mr Wilkins pointed to the door with his ballpoint pen. "Out, boy, out!"

When Jennings had departed, Mr Carter said, "I've no sympathy for Jennings, of course: he deserves all he gets. But it does seem a bit hard on Bromwich."

Mr Wilkins nodded. "I'll let him have his set back in a day or so, when he's finished cutting Jennings down to size," he said. "But I'll do it when it suits *me*. I don't take orders from eleven-year-old boys in Form Three."

Meanwhile, the unfortunate owner of the confiscated radio was touring the school buildings in search of Mr Hind. At length he discovered him in the art-room, trying to decide how best to hang Atkinson's drawing of a party of skiers descending a mountain slope.

Some of the figures portrayed were clearly meant to be standing on their heads, having just collapsed in a snow drift, but others appeared to be skimming across the ski-slope at such unusual angles that the master couldn't tell which way up the picture was intended to be hung.

He looked up as Bromwich came into the room clutching a faded oil painting, fifteen inches across and eight inches high.

"Sir, please, sir, are you an expert on Art?" Bromwich began, coming to a halt just inside the door. "What I mean is, can you just look at a picture and tell whether it's valuable or not?"

"Provided it's not Atkinson's: his art baffles me," the master confessed. "What is it you want to know?"

Bromwich handed him the *Country Scene in Spring*. "There, sir! Would you say that was worth hundreds of pounds?"

Five seconds was time enough for Mr Hind to form his opinion. "No," he said decisively.

"Oh!" Bromwich was disappointed. "Jennings says it's ever so valuable, sir. He says it's an old master."

"Jennings doesn't know the difference between an old master and an old potato," Mr Hind replied. He held the picture at arm's length trying to find something to say in its favour. He even turned it over and studied the back. "Quite a stout piece of canvas," he observed.

Bromwich stared at him with growing concern. "Oh, but, sir, it must be a *bit* priceless," he insisted. "How much would you say it was really worth?"

Once again Mr Hind ran his eye over the painting. Then he said, "Well, if you happened to know anybody who wanted a piece of canvas to patch a hole in an army bell tent, you'd be justified in charging him ten pence. But as a work of art, I'm afraid it has no value at all."

Chapter 9

Blow-up

It was noticed at breakfast on Wednesday, when the post was given out, that there was an unusually large number of letters for Mr Wilkins.

"Birthday cards," Martin-Jones reported, when he returned to the Form Three table after helping to distribute the mail. "You can tell by the shape."

"Old Wilkie having a birthday! I should never have believed it," remarked Temple, churning his porridge into a miniature whirlpool. "Somehow, it's not the sort of thing you'd expect old Sir to do."

"I don't suppose he does it very often – not more than about once a year," said Venables. He looked round, hoping that somebody would think he had said something funny; but everyone was busy eating, and the joke fell flat.

Bromwich was thoughtful as he munched his way through three slices of bread and marmalade. If it was Mr Wilkins' birthday, he ought to be in a good mood, he reasoned. So now was the time to apply the softening-up process necessary for persuading hard-hearted schoolmasters to return confiscated property. It was no good leaving it to Jennings! No good at all!

Jennings had tried chatting Old Wilkie up after lunch on Monday, and a right carve-up he'd made of it! Now, it was up to him – I.K. Bromwich – to see what he could do.

At the moment he had no idea as to how he was going to get into Mr Wilkins' good books, but he wasn't worried. He had the whole day before him, he reminded himself. He'd think of something!

The headmaster announced the plans for the picnic at morning assembly. Needless to say, the news was received with rejoicing.

"Most of you will be going with Mr Carter and Mr Hind," Mr Pemberton-Oakes informed the boys when the cheers had died away. "But I gather from Mr Wilkins, who will be taking the provisions in the mini-bus, that he could do with one or two hard-working helpers to lend a hand with the food baskets."

A sea of hands rose upwards as the whole school simultaneously volunteered for this rewarding work. Transport by mini-bus, it seemed, was considered a better way of travelling than making the journey on two feet. From the seventy-nine volunteers, Mr Pemberton-Oakes chose Johnson, Nuttall, Bromwich and Martin-Jones to make up Mr Wilkins' crew.

At morning break, Mr Wilkins reversed the mini-bus out of the garage, and the willing helpers staggered across the playground with large laundry hampers of food which Matron and Mrs Hackett had prepared in the school kitchen.

Bromwich fired the first shot in his softening-up campaign.

"May I wish you a very happy birthday, sir," he said, beaming with goodwill.

"Thank you," said Mr Wilkins. He was unaware that the pile of envelopes beside his plate at breakfast had provoked comment at the boys' tables. "How did you know?"

"I have my methods, sir." Bromwich switched on a knowing, mysterious smile. "That's why I was glad when the Head chose me to help you with the picnic, sir. I thought it would give me a good chance to make this a very happy day for you, sir."

"Thank you, Bromwich."

"So once again, as I said before, many happy returns and best birthday wishes, sir."

"Thank you, Bromwich."

Martin-Jones gave his colleague a sharp look. It was all very well chatting up Old Wilkie with a spot of flannel to mark the occasion, he thought, but there was no point in laying it on with a trowel.

Johnson and Nuttall arrived with the last of the metal crates containing bottles of fizzy drink.

"There, sir! Eighteen dozen bottles between seventy-nine boys and three masters," Nuttall announced, gasping from his exertions. He closed his eyes, wrestling with a problem of mental arithmetic. "That makes two-point-six-something bottles per head. That won't be enough! We ought to have a few more bottles to make it up to an even number."

Mr Wilkins pulled a face. All forms of fizzy drink were an abomination to him. "You can have my share with pleasure, Nuttall. I wouldn't touch the stuff with a drain-rod, let alone drink it," he said. "Why on earth can't they provide the staff with a decent cup of tea on these occasions, I really don't know."

Jennings was standing nearby with a group of boys

who had come to watch the mini-bus being loaded. At once, his eyebrows shot up in inspiration: Mr Wilkins' remark had sparked off an idea in his mind. He'd have to be quick, though, or it would be too late!

At full speed he raced back across the playground and into the building in search of Darbishire, whom he found changing his shoes in the basement.

"Hey, Darbi! Famous brainwave," he cried excitedly. "I've just thought how we can get some paraffin for our cooking-stove."

"If you think you can get round old Robinson you're wasting your time," Darbishire said, disgustedly. "I happen to know he's got a whole five-gallon drum in the toolshed, but he won't part with a drop."

"Ah, not for *us*, he won't. But if a *master* asked him, he couldn't very well say no, could he?"

The essence of Jennings' plan lay in Mr Wilkins' dislike of fizzy drinks and his yearning for cups of tea on school picnics.

If they were to offer to take Darbishire's camp cooking-stove with them specially to make tea for the staff, they would be certain to earn the undying gratitude of all the masters concerned. With the support of Mr Wilkins, they would be able to borrow a kettle, teapot and other vital equipment from Matron. And Robinson, who always refused favours to third-formers, would have to agree to a request authorized by a master.

"If we've got permission to say Old Wilkie wants it, we can ask him for more paraffin than we need for the picnic, and keep the rest for our camp," Jennings explained.

"M'yes, that's all very well, but if we do that, Sir will know about my stove, and it's supposed to be a secret," Darbishire demurred.

Jennings shrugged. "Well, it's either that, or not being able to use it at all. And anyway, he won't know about the camp, and that's the main thing." He took his friend by the arm and propelled him towards the shoe-lockers. "Get the stove, and then go and ask Old Wilkie, then go and see Robo for the paraffin, and then go and find Matron for the bits and pieces. And then . . ."

"Me! Why always me?" complained Darbishire. "Why not you? It's your famous plan, don't forget."

"Yes, but it's your famous camp stove, don't forget! I very kindly made you a present of it when we gave each other our tennis rackets," his friend reminded him. "So get a move on, or Old Wilkie will have gone before you've had a chance to ask him."

Mr Wilkins was too busy packing the van to pay much attention to what Darbishire was chattering about. Listening with half an ear, he gathered that arrangements could be made to provide the masters with tea instead of fizzy drinks, if they so desired. So naturally he said yes, he'd love a cup, if someone would make it; and then turned his attention again to stacking the bottle crates on the roof-rack.

Armed with this somewhat flimsy permission Darbishire went to the toolshed and assured Robinson that, acting upon Mr Wilkins' instructions, he had come to collect a large bottle of paraffin to make tea for the staff on the picnic. This time, he got his paraffin without argument. Matron, too, co-operated by providing tea, sugar and milk and the necessary utensils; and when the boys finally assembled their equipment on the playground a few minutes later, they felt justified in claiming that the scheme was working well.

The only snag was that Mr Wilkins and his crew had already set off in the mini-bus, which meant that all the tea-making equipment would have to be carried by the walkers. But this was a small price to pay for a bottle of paraffin, most of which would be available for their own use later on.

So Darbishire took the stove, Jennings took the paraffin and the teapot, and other bits and pieces were distributed amongst those of their friends who could be persuaded to lend a hand.

Then, clanking and rattling at every step, the tea-making team joined on to Mr Carter's straggling column and started off on their journey.

After a detour through narrow lanes, and a bumpy climb up the farm track, the mini-bus reached the point at which Mr Wilkins decided to drive no farther. He got out of the driving seat and began lifting down the crates from the roof-rack while his crew unloaded the laundry hampers from inside the van.

It was warm, cheerful work carrying the provisions up the slope to the ridge where they had arranged to meet Mr Carter. Gulls swooped and cried in the clear blue sky and Mr Arrowsmith's sheep, browsing near at hand, scampered away bleating at the working party's approach.

Only one jarring note spoilt this peaceful scene – the sound of Bromwich singing *Happy birthday to you*, slightly off-key. He had been singing it (with variations on the original words) for most of the journey, and by now Mr Wilkins could stand it no longer.

"Oh for goodness sake, boy, *must* you!" he protested, as he followed his crew across the springy turf. "Much as I appreciate your kind wishes, you needn't go *on* and *on* wishing me a very happy birthday – unless you're aiming to give me a very happy nervous breakdown."

"Sorry, sir," the soloist apologized. He'd better be careful, he thought. With so much at stake, it wouldn't do to overplay his hand!

The food hampers were laid out and the bottle crates stood ready to hand when Mr Carter's party arrived, panting and perspiring, at the crest of the hill twenty minutes later. Last to arrive was Darbishire, bowing at the knees under the weight of his cooking-stove which seemed to him to be growing heavier with every step that he took.

Mr Carter made an announcement. "Everybody looks very hot and thirsty, so we'll sit down and have lunch first," he told them. "That'll give you a long afternoon to explore, or play games."

"Or go to sleep," suggested Mr Hind, who was looking forward to a quiet nap in the shade.

"May we have a drink first, please, sir?" Temple asked. "I'm so sizzling hot, I shall go up in smoke in a minute."

"That goes for me, too," Mr Wilkins said, sinking down on the grass. "Didn't I hear somebody say something about a pot of tea for the masters?"

This was Jennings' cue to start his preparations. Assisted by Darbishire and Atkinson, he assembled the tea-making equipment behind a gorse bush some distance away from the main body of picnickers.

"Stove, fuel, kettle, teapot, beakers, bit of stick for a teaspoon, milk, sugar and tea," he said, running his eye over the articles laid out in a semi-circle. "Nothing to light the stove with. Hey, Atki, go and ask one of the masters for a box of matches."

"Bags I be boiler-man," said Darbishire. He uncorked the paraffin and filled the tank of the cooking-stove: in the process he wasted nearly half the contents of the bottle, his wobbling hand sending streams of paraffin running over the top of the stove and dripping down into the teapot standing beside it.

Jennings was furious. "You clumsy great gridiron. Look what you've done!" he stormed, mopping the interior of the teapot with his dirty handkerchief. "Old Wilkie's not going to say thank you for a cup of tea tasting of paraffin."

"I couldn't help it. It's this stupid bottle: it needs a funnel," the boiler-man defended himself.

"Yes, but look how much you've wasted. There won't be enough over for use next Sunday."

"Of course there will! The stove's overflowing up to the brim, now. We shan't use all that, just boiling one kettle."

Atkinson returned with Mr Hind's matches and Jennings replaced the teapot beside the stove and applied a light to the gauze pad under the burner.

He backed away quickly as flames a foot high shot into the air, and little bonfires broke out in the surrounding grass where the paraffin was still dripping down on to the turf.

"Wow! Help! It's out of control," Darbishire cried in alarm.

"Don't panic. It's only where it's flooded: it'll soon settle down," Jennings assured him.

Leaving the stove to burn up its surplus fuel, the three boys ran round stamping on the tufts of burning grass before the fire could gain a hold. By the time they had finished, the stove appeared to have righted itself, but by now flames were coming out of the teapot where Jennings' handkerchief, having soaked up some of the paraffin, was acting as a makeshift wick.

Atkinson rushed to cope with this new outbreak. Finding the teapot too hot to handle, he kicked it over on its side and poked out the flaming handkerchief with the aid of a stick.

"Whew! It should be a good cup of tea when it's ready, seeing all the trouble we're going to," he observed, beating the smouldering remains of the handkerchief with his shoe.

He glanced back at the picnic site, surprised that nobody had come rushing across to see what was happening; but the three masters were busy unpacking the lunch baskets, and everybody else seemed too absorbed in their own affairs to pay much attention to the scene of chaos behind the gorse bush. "OK then, Jennings. Put the kettle on, or old Sir won't get his tea till lighting-up time."

Jennings picked up the kettle, and at once a look of incredulous horror shot into his eyes. "Oh fish-hooks!" he cried in dismay. *"We haven't got any water?"*

They stared at him in disbelief. "You're joking! Of *course* we've got some water. We *must* have." For a moment, Darbishire's mind refused to accept the inevitable. Then he squawked, *"Why* haven't we got any water?"

"Because nobody's brought any – that's why," Jennings retorted angrily. He racked his brains for a scapegoat. "It's Venables' fault! He was carrying the kettle. He never said it was empty."

"Why should he? You were supposed to be in charge," Atkinson pointed out. "He probably thought someone else had got the water."

"Yes, but all the same, you'd think he would have—"

Jennings broke off and flipped his fingers in exasperation. There was no denying the fact that he himself was wholly to blame. "Where can we get some from?" he demanded.

"Dig a well," Atkinson suggested. He could afford to treat the disaster lightly: as a mere helper, he was not so involved in the operation as the two principals.

"Don't be funny: this is serious," said Darbishire. "We can't go all the way back to school for a kettleful, and there just isn't any other water for miles around. We'll have to scrap the idea: it's impossible."

Even when faced with the impossible, Jennings was reluctant to admit defeat. Deep in thought, he stood scowling at the empty kettle for a few moments, and then said, "How would it be if we used fizzy lemonade instead of water?"

Darbishire snorted in derision. "Hopeless! They'd notice it at the first mouthful."

"Not if they were really thirsty. We could make the tea extra strong and put in lashings of sugar and milk to hide the taste," Jennings argued. "Come on, let's go and get a few bottles out of the crate. I could do with a drink myself."

"So could I – but not boiled," said Atkinson. "It's going to be a funny pot of tea when it's ready," he went on, as he and Jennings turned and trotted across to the picnic site together. "Hot fizzy lemonade on tea leaves flavoured with paraffin – not to mention a few specks of burnt handkerchief floating on the top."

Darbishire remained behind for a few moments to satisfy himself that the cooking-stove was working properly. The flame round the boiling ring was still burning brightly, he noticed, but something unusual – and indeed frightening – was happening to the fuel tank . . . Blisters of paint were forming on the metal sides – blisters that swelled up and burst as he watched. Alarmed, Darbishire turned and ran off to report the latest development without delay.

He found Jennings and Atkinson by the crates trying to decide whether to make the tea with cherryade or orange squash.

"Hey! *Hey!* Emergency!" the messenger shrilled, skidding to a halt beside them. "Something funny's happening to the stove – *it's glowing!*"

"How d'you mean?"

"The fuel tank's red hot and blowing paint bubbles. I reckon it's – sort of – lit back on itself and the whole tank's alight inside."

"Why didn't you switch the thing off, then?"

"I couldn't: it was too hot. And, anyway, I daren't touch it because I thought it might—"

Darbishire broke off as a deafening report rent the air from behind the distant gorse bush . . . The cooking stove had blown itself to smithereens.

The entire party of seventy-nine boys and three masters leaped with shock as the detonation thundered about their ears. Bottles of fizzy drink dropped from nerveless fingers, and mouths that had opened to take a bite of ham sandwich remained agape in stunned confusion. Some boys threw themselves flat on their faces in self-preservation; others fell over their own feet in sheer surprise. For some moments all was turmoil and

The cooking-stove had blown itself to smithereens.

confusion. Gulls squawked and panicked overhead, and sheep stampeded on the nearby slopes.

When the shock wave had died away, an excited barrage of questions and comments broke from the lips of the picnickers.

Most of the boys were convinced that a bomb had dropped close at hand; others toyed with the idea of a subterranean explosion of natural gas. Binns and Blotwell (keen readers of science fiction) formed a fascinating theory about a crash-landing of a Martian space-ship manned by little green men with eight arms and legs.

Jennings was able to dispel the rumours and set everyone's mind at rest.

"It's all right. It's only our cooking-stove," he reported, pointing to the distant gorse bush. "It's blown up."

"Just as we were going to make the masters a lovely cup of tea," Darbishire added, coyly.

There was a rush towards the gorse bush to inspect the scene of the accident, but Mr Carter called the boys back and confined them to the area of the picnic site. Then, he and Mr Wilkins went over to find out what had happened and make sure that no further danger existed.

They returned a few minutes later, having extinguished a small fire round the roots of the gorse bush and gathered up a few pieces of broken crockery and a badly-dented kettle which was all that remained of the tea-making equipment.

"It's a good thing nobody was near it when it went off," Mr Carter told Mr Hind, when the investigators rejoined the party. "It was my fault, really. I should have known better than to let Jennings and Darbishire bring that thing with them." He sighed and shook his head. "They're not fit to be left in charge of an electric toothbrush – let alone an antiquated contraption like that cooking-stove."

Mr Wilkins forced a wan smile. "And *I* should have known better than to look forward to a nice cup of tea," he observed. "Things like that don't happen on school picnics – not the sort that *I* go on, anyway."

Seated on the grass a short distance away, Jennings and Darbishire were munching ham rolls and slaking their thirst with fizzy lemonade. The accident had left them subdued in spirit, and for a while they ate in silence.

Then Jennings said, "Well, at least we've got one thing to be thankful for, Darbi. If it hadn't exploded when it did, we should be spending half the afternoon trying to explain to Old Wilkie why his tea tasted of orange squash and paraffin."

Darbishire scratched his nose thoughtfully. "Yes, it's let us off the hook nicely, hasn't it!" he agreed.

Chapter 10

Prehistoric Joke

With the prospect of a long, hot afternoon before them, Mr Carter insisted upon all the boys taking a short rest after the picnic lunch. So they spread themselves on the grass in little groups and discussed how they proposed to spend the time that lay before them.

Naturally enough, Jennings and Darbishire planned to busy themselves at their camp which was less than a quarter of a mile away in the heart of the gorse-bush jungle. Despite the fact that camp cookery would now have to be crossed off their list of activities, there still remained a hundred things that an enterprising explorer could find to do in a cave dwelling off the beaten track.

"I had a look at your famous prehistoric paintings when I went up there to get our things on Monday," Jennings remarked, lying on his stomach and chewing a head of clover. "They're not at all bad, really. I bet lots of people would think they were real, if they didn't look too closely."

"Honestly?" Darbishire glowed with pride. "Mr Hind, for instance?"

"Well, perhaps not him, because he knows all about

114

Art. He's seen the genuine article at the Lascaux caves and places," Jennings amended. "But I bet you could fool anybody who wasn't an expert."

This was high praise, indeed – especially coming from Jennings, who normally greeted his friend's artistic efforts with derision. Darbishire was delighted: if old Jen thought his paintings could pass muster, it might be a bit of fun to put the theory to the test.

"Shall we try – just for a joke?" he suggested, sitting upright and looking around for likely victims. "Suppose we got – say – Temple and Venables to come and explore with us in the bushes, and then let them discover the cave all by themselves." His eyes sparkled with mischief as the idea took shape in his mind. "They'd think they'd stumbled across some genuine prehistoric paintings that have been there since the Stone Age."

Jennings shook with helpless laughter. "Fantastic wheeze! And we'll pretend we've never seen the cave before, so they won't think we had anything to do with it."

"And they'll go rushing back to tell the masters and everybody—"

"And everybody will say they're talking through their hats. And *they'll* say, 'Come and see for yourselves, if you don't believe us'—"

"And everybody will go flocking—" Darbishire broke off as a snag occurred to him. "Ah yes, but we don't want the masters knowing where the cave is, or it won't be secret any more."

There was a pause while Jennings considered the objection. Then he said, "Fair enough! We'll wait till the expedition is ready to set off to inspect ye most famous discovery of all time, and then we'll tell them it's an April Fool in July, so they needn't bother to go."

The conspirators lay back on the grass trying to stifle their laughter and envisage the climax of their hoax.

"I can see it all," Darbishire gurgled happily. "Us standing there laughing our heads off, and Venables and Temple – or whoever it is – hopping with rage when they find out we've been taking the mickey out of them."

A few minutes later Mr Carter announced the end of the rest period, and the picnickers got to their feet, eager to start the afternoon's activities.

Several of the boys set off with cameras or insect-boxes; others made for the crest of the hill to launch model gliders. Complicated games of kidnap, rescue and escape, in and around the gorse bushes, had been arranged during the siesta and, in addition, teams had been picked for cricket and rounders on open patches of grassland. Indeed, most of the boys had a full programme of events to keep them busy during the afternoon.

"Quick, Darbi! We've got to get hold of them before they mooch off and do something else," Jennings said, jumping up as soon as Mr Carter had finished speaking. "And mind you keep a straight face when we ask them. We don't want to arouse their suspicions."

"Righto – old poker-face, that's me!" Darbishire practised keeping his face straight as he got to his feet, but the effort made him squint. He said, "How would it be if we told them that some famous professor has proved that a tribe of cave-dwellers used to live around these parts a million years ago?"

"We'll tell them that *after* they've found the paintings

– not before," Jennings decided. "It's too much of a good thing to walk *slap-bang* into a cave full of art treasures by chance, just after someone's told you about it. Even an addle-pated clodpoll like Temple would think it fishy if you laid it on as thick as that."

Venables and Temple had not made any definite plans for the afternoon, so they were quite willing to fall in with Jennings' suggestion to go exploring in the thickest parts of the gorse jungle.

In a matter of minutes they had left the open downland behind them and were forcing their way through the undergrowth, following the track taken by Jennings and Darbishire on their first visit to the cave.

To begin with, they had to crawl on hands and knees, but after a while the branches thinned and they were able to walk upright. By this time they had reached the copse where, ten days before, Mr Arrowsmith's wandering ewe had been held fast by a fallen branch.

Darbishire recognized the spot at once. "Hey, Jen, see where we are! It was just about here that—"

He caught his friend's warning look and stopped abruptly. The hoax demanded that this should be new territory to all four of the explorers. Fortunately, Venables and Temple were examining an alleged fox-hole and had not noticed Darbishire's indiscretion.

A hundred yards farther on they came into the clearing where, to their left, the ground curved away to the valley. On their right was the upward slope of the steeply rising hillside with the cave mouth just discernible in the shadow.

Here, Jennings halted the party and looked about

him. "This might be a good place to explore," he said, casually.

"Too hot," retorted Temple, collapsing on the grass. "Let's have a rest."

"But we've just had one! We've only just got up from sitting down after lunch."

Temple shrugged. "OK then, you go ahead and explore. I'm all right where I am, thanks."

Jennings changed his tactics. "Hey, Venables," he said, pointing up the hillside, "D'you reckon anyone could climb that slope without going on all fours?"

Venables sat down beside his friend. "Easy – if they'd got the energy. Me – I'm puffed!"

It was obvious to the conspirators that their victims would not walk into the trap without a push in the right direction. So after a few minutes of aimless conversation, Jennings suddenly said, "I spy with my little eye something beginning with *C*."

"Clouds," said Temple, staring up at the sky.

"Clover," said Venables, spiking a leaf with his penknife.

"Crocodile," said Darbishire, aiming wide for safety.

Jennings shook his head. "Cave," he told them. "At least it *looks* like a cave from here."

They followed the direction of his pointing finger and agreed that he might well be right. However, they showed no particular interest in verifying the fact for themselves.

The next move came from Darbishire. He gave a convincing little shudder and said, "I shouldn't fancy going into a cave like that, all by myself. Might be a bit scary."

The intended victims exchanged superior glances.

They had never held a very high opinion of Darbishire as a man of action.

"Frightened?" Temple inquired with gentle malice.

With an effort, Darbishire managed to assume his straight face. "Well, just a bit. So would you be."

Temple guffawed in derision. "*Me*! Scared of a mouldy old cave!"

"Go on, then," Darbishire pointed up the hill. "I dare you . . . I challenge you . . . I challenge *both* of you!"

The ruse worked perfectly. Venables and Temple set off up the slope like a couple of mountain hares, while the two conspirators hid their faces and stuffed their fingers into their mouths to muffle the gales of laughter welling up inside them.

"Well done, Darbi!" Jennings gasped, when his mirth was under control. "We've got them properly on the hook, now."

"And I kept a straight face, didn't I! Even though I was just about bursting."

"Yes, well, mind you go on keeping it straight when they come out again. We don't want to give the game away till we're ready."

By now, Venables and Temple were clambering up the steepest part of the slope, just below the entrance to the cave. The conspirators followed at a safe distance, anxious to be within earshot when their victims came rushing out to announce their dramatic discovery of prehistoric art.

"We'll pretend to be absolutely flabbergasted," Jennings said, as they made their way up the lower slopes of the bank.

"Yes, of course!" Darbishire practised a few random

119

exclamations indicating astonishment. "Wow! Gosh! Fossilised fish-hooks! Goodness gracious! Fancy that! Well I never! Did you ever!"

"All right, all right. Don't overdo it," Jennings said curtly.

Halfway up the slope the two boys came to a stop and squatted on the grass to await developments. Above, they could see Venables and Temple stooping down to crawl through the low entrance to the cave.

"Now we shan't be long!" said Jennings.

He was right! . . . For in less than ten seconds cries of terror and alarm rang out from within the cave, and the next moment Venables and Temple shot out through the cave mouth, falling over each other in their desperate efforts to get back into the light of day. Panic-stricken, they slithered down the bank, eyes staring, mouths gaping and gibbering with shock.

There was no need for Jennings and Darbishire to *pretend* to be flabbergasted: their astonishment was genuine. Something had obviously gone wrong with the hoax.

"Hey! Whoa! What's going on?" Jennings shouted, stepping into his companions' path to stop their downward rush. "What's the matter with you? Have you gone mad?"

They checked their flight and stumbled to a halt, but for some seconds they were incapable of speech.

Then Temple jerked a trembling finger at the scene of their ordeal and squawked, "It's in there . . . Inside the cave . . . We heard it!"

"Heard what?" Darbishire demanded.

"I don't know. The *thing*! Groaning and wailing and grinding his teeth."

Venables and Temple shot out through the cave mouth.

"And beating on the walls to get out," Venables added with a shudder.

"What are you talking about? *What's* inside the cave? What did you see?" Jennings' voice was shrill, as the contagion of panic spread to all four members of the group.

"We don't know. We couldn't see anything. The noise was coming from inside the rock. It might have been a man . . . It might have been a body."

"Well, it couldn't have been a *dead* one, if he was moaning and grinding his teeth," Darbishire pointed out.

"It could if he was a ghost. He was wailing like a banshee and probably rattling his chains as well, only I didn't wait to listen. I got out pretty quick."

Pale with shock, Venables did his best to fill in the details. He and Temple had been laughing together as they had scrambled over the threshold, but, once inside, terror had struck. The cave was empty, but eerie, unearthly sounds were coming out of the tunnel leading into the chalk. Someone or something was lurking within!

Jennings suddenly felt weak at the knees. He, himself, might have met the thing – whatever it was – face to face, when he had been exploring the tunnel. He'd had a lucky escape! Even to look back upon, it was a frightening thought.

For a split second it crossed his mind that the story might be a hoax – the same sort of hoax that he and Darbishire had been planning at their companions' expense. But a moment's thought convinced him that the terror was genuine. Unlike Darbishire before them, Temple and Venables had no need to assume a straight face for the sake of appearances: the look in their eyes was proof enough that they had just undergone a harrowing ordeal.

Darbishire glanced nervously over his shoulder, measuring the distance up the slope to the mouth of the cave.

"D'you think it's safe standing here like this?" he queried. "I can't hear anything, but—"

"Of course you can't hear anything down *here*," Temple snapped irritably. "You go and stick your head inside if you want to know what it sounds like."

"No, thanks. I'll take your word for it," Darbishire said with a gulp.

Jennings made a quick decision. "Come on! We'll go and tell Mr Carter. He'll know what to do."

He turned and started running down the bank to the gap in the bushes through which they had reached the clearing. The others followed close on his heels, fearful in their minds, yet thankful at the prospect of sharing the perils of the unknown with a responsible adult.

Panting and breathless, they made their way back through the undergrowth. No one felt like speaking, and only the crackling of brushwood underfoot and the swirl of branches as they forced their way past, disturbed the silence of the afternoon.

When at last they broke from the cover of the gorse and ran full speed to the picnic site, it was as though they were emerging into a different world – a normal, orderly world, untroubled by fears and mysteries that they could not understand . . .

Mr Wilkins was playing French cricket with Bromwich and Rumbelow. Mr Carter was chatting to Mr Arrowsmith who had walked up from the farm. Mr Hind was asleep in the shade of a gorse bush: behind the bush crouched Binns and Blotwell blowing up a paper bag with which to blast him into wakefulness. Atkinson was pulling his face into grotesque contortions as he posed for Martin-Jones to take a photograph. Form Four were playing Form Five at rounders. Johnson was wrestling with Nuttall. Pettigrew was practising handstands . . . Everyone was behaving normally: the explorers were back in the world they knew!

Jennings was the first to reach Mr Carter. "Sir, sir! Emergency, sir. Come quickly!" he shrilled.

Mr Carter was about to reprimand him for interrupting his conversation, but Jennings' urgent tone and worried look caused him to change his mind. With a word of apology to Mr Arrowsmith, he turned and said, "What is it, Jennings? Has there been an accident?"

"Yes sir. A ghastly accident, sir, but not to one of our lot. It's a mysterious stranger, sir, trapped in a cave."

Venables and Temple, as chief witnesses, had been hoping to announce the shattering news themselves. They were furious with Jennings for butting in before they had had a chance to make themselves heard.

"*We'll* tell you what happened, Venables and me. Jennings wasn't even there, sir," Temple retorted.

"Yes, I was. I was just outside."

"Ah, but we were a lot closer. We actually heard him, moaning and groaning like a ghost and making terrible throat noises, as though he was being strangled."

"And kicking and struggling and beating on the walls to get out," Venables added. "So we came as fast as we could to tell you, sir."

It took Mr Carter a few minutes to make sense of

the garbled information. When he had sorted out fact from fiction as best he could, he said, "Right! I'll go and have a look. You boys come with me and point out where this cave is."

"I'll come along, too," Mr Arrowsmith volunteered. "If it's half as bad as these lads are trying to make out, you'll need someone to lend you a hand."

With a brief word of explanation to Mr Hind (now wide awake, thanks to the detonations of Binns and Blotwell), Mr Carter set off with his party to investigate the mystery.

In the gorse-bush jungle Jennings was the pathfinder, and under his guidance the group made their way to the clearing.

"There, sir, that's the place," he said, pointing uphill to the fault in the rock. And Mr Arrowsmith scratched his head and said, "That's odd! It's right on the edge of my grazing land, but I never noticed there was a cave there before."

On hands and knees they clambered up the slope, the two men in the lead. By now the boys were no longer feeling frightened, for, with a master to take charge, their fears had given place to a fever of curiosity to know what the search would reveal.

All was quiet as they climbed the slope, but when they reached the entrance to the cave they could hear the noise coming from within – a noise which grew in volume as they stopped at the threshold to listen.

The sound was difficult to identify – a mixture of scraping, banging and hoarse grunts of distress.

"What on earth is it?" Temple whispered, his fears returning with a rush.

"I don't know, but I'll soon find out," Mr Carter

said. He crawled through the opening and stared at the mouth of the tunnel from which the sounds were coming. "Pity we haven't got a torch. We'll have to make do with matches."

He was fumbling in his pocket when Mr Arrowsmith suddenly said, "Hey, just a minute! Do you mind if I go in first?"

"Why?"

"I've just had a thought. I may be wrong, but if my theory's on target I reckon I'd be able to cope with the problem more easily than you. More my line of country, if you see what I mean."

The two men changed places, and Mr Arrowsmith lay flat on the ground and wormed his way into the tunnel. He was a big man with broad shoulders, and the confined space was a handicap to one of his build. Whereas Jennings had been able to make his way on hands and knees, the farmer was obliged to lie flat on his stomach and inch himself forward.

As the boys watched from the cave mouth, the first match sparked, flared up and died in the darkness.

"Can't see a thing," Mr Arrowsmith's voice floated back from the passage. "But I'm pretty sure I'm on the right track."

When the next match was struck he had penetrated several yards of darkness, and the watchers could see nothing but the soles of his boots. As he went farther into the tunnel the match-head lights grew fainter, and soon no glimmer reached the cave mouth: but still the baffling noises went on.

Suddenly the sounds ceased, only to break out again a moment later in frantic pandemonium. Then came Mr Arrowsmith's voice, his tone reassuring though the words were inaudible. After that, came sounds of struggle and scuffling, and then the scraping of the farmer's boots on the chalk as he began his retreat into the daylight.

It seemed a long time to the watchers in the cave before the soles of Mr Arrowsmith's boots could be seen edging backwards towards the open end of the passage. Unable to turn round, he was coming out feet first, lying on his stomach and dragging something after him. What it was they couldn't see, for their view was blocked by the farmer's body; but they could hear him gasping and struggling with the effort of heaving his burden back into the daylight.

At last he emerged from the tunnel, dragging behind him a frightened Southdown sheep.

The boys' first reaction was a mixture of surprise and relief. Fear of the unknown had set their minds flitting from one alarming fantasy to another. Now, they could stop teasing their imaginations and be thankful that the situation was resolved. At the same time, they couldn't help feeling disappointed that what had promised to be a baffling mystery had turned out to be something of a damp squib.

Mr Arrowsmith was so exhausted by his work of rescue that he sank down on the cave floor in a state of near-collapse.

"I guessed it was my stupid old maverick up to her tricks when I heard the row she was kicking up," he gasped, mopping his brow with his handkerchief. "Goodness knows how or why she got herself into that tunnel, but one thing I *do* know: she'd never have got out again by herself. She'd fallen into a sort of pit where the ground gives way at the far end."

Jennings remembered the pit at the end of the tunnel, but he didn't say anything. This was hardly the moment, he thought, to entertain the party with an account of his pot-holing activities.

The wandering ewe seemed little the worse for her experience for as soon as the farmer had released his hold she darted out of the cave and began browsing on the slope beyond the entrance.

"Just as well you lads heard her, or it would have been the end of old Mrs Maverick," Mr Arrowsmith said, as he got to his feet. "She may have been stuck there for the last three or four days, for all we know."

When the farmer had recovered his breath, the rescue party crawled out of the cave and set off on the homeward trek. With some difficulty they managed to drive the sheep before them through the undergrowth, and when they reached the open downland Mr Arrowsmith was able to take on the job single-handed, and return his straying ewe to the flock which was grazing nearby.

All the way back through the jungle, Darbishire had been deep in thought. Now that the mystery of the cave had been resolved, his mind kept returning to the hoax which had set the rescue operation in motion. Given the chance, would the trick have worked, or wouldn't it? He could hardly wait to find out!

So when Mr Carter and the boys sat down to regain their breath at the picnic site, Darbishire chose a seat between Venables and Temple. Casually, he said, "By the way, what did you lot think of those rather unusual paintings we saw in the cave?"

"Paintings? What paintings? I didn't see any paintings," said Temple.

"Oh but surely, you *must* have done! I thought they were really interesting, didn't you, Venables?"

"I don't know. I didn't notice them. Why? What was so special about them?"

Darbishire heaved a sigh of resignation. "Oh, nothing! Forget it!" he said in a dull, flat voice . . . If ever a practical joke had fallen flat on its face, it was the hoax of the primitive cave paintings!

Chapter 11

Restricted Access

At six o'clock, when the last ham roll had been eaten and the last bottle of fizzy drink had been drained, Mr Carter gave the order to set off for home.

"We'll leave Mr Wilkins' crew behind to pack the mini-bus," he told them when the whole party had gathered at the picnic site. "The rest of you can start walking, now."

"Sir, please may I walk, too?" Martin-Jones asked. "I want to go back with Pettigrew because we're in the middle of an important discussion about—"

"All right," Mr Carter agreed. "We'll find someone to take your place on the bus crew."

Jennings' hand was the first to shoot up, so Mr Carter chose him from the flood of volunteers anxious to avoid the effort of returning to school on their own two feet.

It was easy work carrying the empty containers back to the bus when the rest of the school had departed. The crew stacked the hampers inside, while Mr Wilkins heaved the metal bottle crates on to the roof-rack and secured them with straps. Then the boys climbed aboard and the vehicle bumped and rattled its way down the rough farm track.

Bromwich sat next to Mr Wilkins and did his best to

earn the master's approval by steering the conversation round to the topic that had occupied him on the outward journey.

"Talking about birthdays, they say that seven years of a dog's life are equal to one year of a person's," he began. "So I was just thinking of all the presents and all the birthday cakes you'd have had, if you'd been born a dog instead of a person. Almost makes you wish you had, doesn't it, sir!"

"You speak for yourself. I'll settle for being born human," the driver retorted.

"Yes, all right, sir. But talking about presents, I had a pocket radio for my birthday, only Jennings borrowed it when I was in the sick-room." Bromwich paused hopefully, but Mr Wilkins didn't rise to the bait, so he went on, "I heard ever such a funny joke about a month ago. There was this man who had a dog, you see, and he said to his friend . . ."

The terrible joke led to more terrible jokes; and in the rear of the van the rest of the boys were singing untunefully at the tops of their voices. Mr Wilkins couldn't decide whether the jokes or the singing grated the worse upon his long-suffering ears.

However, with the exception of the driver, the party were in high spirits all the way back to school. It was only when they had reached their destination and were within a yard of journey's end, that something sensational happened . . .

At a brisk thirty-five miles per hour the mini-bus sailed up the drive, heading for the garage at the far end of the playground. The garage doors were standing open, so Mr Wilkins decided to drive straight in before disembarking his passengers.

But as the vehicle crossed the threshold there was a sudden crunch, a shuddering jolt, the engine stalled and the bus stopped dead in its tracks, throwing the passengers out of their seats. Shaken, but unhurt, the boys picked themselves up off the floor.

"Wow! We've crashed! What did we hit?" Johnson cried in alarm.

Mr Wilkins released his safety-belt and jumped out of the driving seat while the passengers shot out through the rear doors to discover what had happened . . . The mini-bus was stuck in the entrance, half in and half out of the garage doors.

The cause of the accident was plain to see. There was enough headroom to admit the vehicle with a foot to spare – but not with the crates of empty bottles strapped to the roof-rack! Now the bus was held fast by a solid metal wedge driven home tightly between the brick lintel of the doorway and the roof of the vehicle.

"Oh, *no*!" Mr Wilkins clapped his hand to his brow in dismay. It was his own fault, of course. If only he had remembered those wretched crates in time!

The passengers, though sympathetic, were unable to suppress a certain pleasure at being involved in a mishap for which no one could hold *them* to blame.

"Bad luck, sir. Really bad luck!" Jennings consoled him.

"And on your birthday, too," Bromwich added with deep concern. "It's a good job you and I were wearing our seat belts, wasn't it, sir!"

"Do you think you'll be able to get it free, sir?" Johnson asked. "Or will you have to take the garage down, brick by brick?"

Nuttall giggled and said, "Poor old Martin-Jones!

I bet he wouldn't have given up his place if he'd known he was going to miss this!"

They lined up just clear of the garage doors, watching with interest as the driver tried to weigh up the problem that faced him. A quick inspection showed that the vehicle had sustained no damage. That was something to be thankful for, but it didn't answer the question of how to release it from the vice-like grip in which it was held.

Mr Wilkins unfastened the straps on the roof-rack, but he was unable to move either the crates or the rack in any direction.

It was infuriating, he thought! If only the crates had been an inch shorter, the accident would never have happened. Had they been an inch taller they would have hit the brickwork above the doorway and stopped the bus from entering. As it was, the vehicle's own momentum had forced it a few feet beyond the threshold, ramming home the wedge which was causing all the trouble.

Baffled, Mr Wilkins got back into the driver's seat and started the engine in the hope of propelling the vehicle backwards by its own power. It was useless! He might as well have tried to drive it through a stone wall.

He was wondering what to do next when the headmaster strolled across the playground to exchange a few words with the master in charge of the working-party.

"Safely back, I see!" he observed genially, as he reached the garage. "I trust that all went well on the picnic."

The look on Mr Wilkins' face informed him that whatever may, or may not, have happened on the picnic, all was not going well at the present moment.

"I'm terribly sorry, HM, but I've had a slight accident," the master explained, pointing to the roof-rack. "We're stuck under the lintel. Jammed tight! I can't budge it, one way or the other."

Mr Pemberton-Oakes was horrified. "Good heavens! This is terrible! Well, really, Wilkins, I do think you might have exercised a little more care." His concern was understandable, for the vehicle was almost new.

"It's all right. There's no actual damage – *yet.* The roof-rack's stopping the crates from going through the top." Mr Wilkins gave a little, apologetic laugh. "It's just that I don't see how we're going to release it."

"Oh, but surely! There *must* be a way!" the headmaster insisted.

He went inside the garage to check the truth of his assistant's forebodings. He tugged at the crates without success; he unscrewed the fastenings of the roof-rack to no good purpose. He, too, put the bus into gear and was unable to make it move. At length he came out of the garage looking very worried.

"I'm afraid you're right, Wilkins. The position is extremely serious. I can't think what we can do. I don't see what *anyone* can do."

Mr Wilkins racked his brains for an idea. "Perhaps we could saw through the crates," he suggested.

"Impossible! There isn't enough room to manoeuvre a saw. And even if we tried, the pressure from above wouldn't allow us to slide the pieces clear." Mr Pemberton-Oakes shook his head in despair. "I honestly don't see how we're going to move the bus without dismantling the garage."

Johnson turned to Nuttall in triumph and whispered,

"There you are! I told you! I said they'd have to take it down, brick by brick, didn't I."

All this time, Jennings had been standing on the edge of the group, staring at the stranded vehicle and thinking hard. Now he came forward with hand raised to attract the masters' attention.

"Sir, please, sir, I've had a brainwave," he began.

"Be quiet, boy," Mr Wilkins snapped irritably. "Can't you see the Head and I have got a problem on our hands! We haven't got time to waste listening to stupid suggestions at a time like this."

"Oh, but it's not stupid, sir, honestly. I just thought that—"

"We don't want to hear it, whatever it is," Mr Wilkins retorted. "Run away, Jennings! You can't help, and that's that."

"Yes, all right, sir," Jennings agreed. He half-turned to join his companions. "I was only going to say that if you let the air out of all the tyres, the bus would sink about three inches, so the doorway wouldn't be pressing on it, any more."

Mr Pemberton-Oakes was a man who seldom betrayed his feelings by the expression on his face. But now his eyebrows shot up and his eyes opened wide in instant appreciation of this inspired piece of reasoning.

"By jove, he's right, Wilkins!" he exclaimed in admiration. "It's the obvious answer. Well done, Jennings! I congratulate you upon your initiative."

Mr Wilkins responded with a wan smile. He was wishing that he hadn't been so hasty in condemning Jennings' brainwave before he'd heard the details. However, he lost no time in putting the plan into operation.

He hurried round from wheel to wheel, unscrewing the tyre valves.

The brainwave worked! There was a loud hissing as the compressed air escaped from the tyres. As it did so, the mini-bus slowly subsided until it was standing on its wheel-rims. When the four tyres were flat there was a space of more than two inches between the top of the metal crates and the brick lintel of the doorway.

Very slowly, Mr Wilkins backed the bus out of the garage and then set to work removing the containers from the roof.

"Thank goodness for that! I thought we were going to be in real trouble," the headmaster said with a sigh of relief, as he watched the van being unloaded. He smiled encouragingly at the instigator of the brainwave. "Good work, Jennings! It just shows what you can do when you really apply your mind to a problem."

By this time, the rest of the picnic party were straggling in through the bottom gate and making their way up to school across the playing-fields.

"Ah, that reminds me! I must have a word with Carter," Mr Pemberton-Oakes went on. He nodded briefly to the perspiring Mr Wilkins. "By the way, you'll see the bus is all ready to use before you go indoors, won't you! My car's being serviced, so I shall need it to go into Dunhambury this evening."

As the headmaster strode away, Bromwich made yet another attempt to inch his way into Mr Wilkins' favour.

"Oh, bad luck, sir. What really bad luck! All that trouble and now you've got to pump the beastly tyres up again!" He sighed in sympathy. "What a thing to happen on your birthday! Would you like me to help you, sir? I could—"

"No, I wouldn't," Mr Wilkins said curtly. "Run away, boy, run away!" He'd had enough of Bromwich and his kind wishes to last him till his *next* birthday, he told himself!

Despite the master's discouraging tone, Bromwich refused to give up hope. Admittedly, the task of chatting up Mr Wilkins was proving more difficult than he'd thought, but surely there must be some way of getting into the master's good books: otherwise, he'd *never* get his radio back!

Deep in thought, Bromwich walked across the playground to the main building. How would it be, he wondered, if he were to give Mr Wilkins a present – a *birthday* present? . . . H'm! The problem was to think of a suitable gift.

Mr Wilkins didn't collect foreign stamps or matchbox labels, either of which Bromwich would have been happy to provide. It was also known that the master didn't like mint humbugs or chewing-gum, and he'd already got a better pen than the tatty old cracked one with a faulty flow that Bromwich would have been willing to sacrifice in a good cause.

So what else could he give him?

Frowning with concentration, Bromwich went down to the basement to search his tuck-box for suitable gifts. He lifted the lid and peered inside, and at once his eyes lit up with inspiration.

Why, of course! It was just the thing! . . . Not even Mr Wilkins could fail to take the hint when presented with such a valuable gift!

*

A light supper was served for the school at half-past seven, and shortly after the meal was over the dormitory bell signalled the end of a long and tiring day.

Mr Wilkins was the master on duty that evening. He, too, had had a long and tiring day. Inflating the mini-bus tyres had provided a strenuous climax to an energetic afternoon, and he was looking forward to relaxing in an armchair as soon as the boys were in bed and he had called silence in the dormitories.

On the second floor landing he met Jennings emerging from the bathroom in his pyjamas, his hair dripping wet and his toothbrush clenched between his teeth like a tobacco pipe.

"Hullo, sir," Jennings greeted him, wide-eyed and smiling. He removed the toothbrush. "It was a good job I was able to help you when the bus got stuck, wasn't it! It was my chance to – sort of – do you a good turn, as you might say."

Mr Wilkins acknowledged the good turn with a gracious smile.

"And to do the whole school a good turn, really, sir. Especially the Head. It would have cost hundreds of pounds if he'd had to have the garage taken apart, wouldn't it!"

Mr Wilkins conceded the point. "Yes, very probably."

"I always like doing people good turns," Jennings went on, looking up at the master with the eager innocence of a spaniel begging for a bone. "That's why I was trying to do one for Bromwich the other day when I came to see you about – er – well, you know—"

"All right, all right! I can take a hint," Mr Wilkins broke in with a laugh. It was obvious where the conversation was leading. "I've had plenty of practice today. Bromwich has been dropping hints like high-explosive bombs ever since morning break, so there's no need for you to start sniping at me, as well." He paused for a moment and added, "Very well then, Jennings. You can present my compliments to Bromwich and tell him that if he comes to my room after breakfast tomorrow, he may hear something to his advantage."

"Thank you, sir. Thank you very much indeed, sir. You've done me a good turn, too, as well as Bromwich, because now I shall be able to get my security back."

"Your – *what*?"

"Oh, nothing, sir. Nothing important, really. Just a little business matter between me and old Bromo. Goodnight, sir."

Thrusting his toothbrush back between his jaws, Jennings passed on down the landing, well satisfied with the encounter. It wasn't too difficult to chat up old Sir, he thought, if you played your cards right.

When Mr Wilkins eventually reached his sitting-room after staff supper that evening, he found a flat rectangular package awaiting him on the table.

Inside was a faded oil painting entitled *Country Scene in Spring* which, if he had measured it (which he didn't), he would have found to be fifteen inches in length by eight in height. There was also a note in letters of red and blue ball-point saying:

To Mr Wilkins. Wishing you a happy birthday and many of them.

Yours truly,

I.K. Bromwich.

PS. This picture is not so valuable as people thought, but it is a bit valuable all the same. I.K.B.

PPS. Latest joke! When you have had a lot more birthdays you will be an Old Master, like this picture. End of joke. I.K.B.

The joke raised no smile on Mr Wilkins' lips and the old master inspired no joy in his heart. The picture was, if anything, even worse than the joke.

It had, moreover, been given to him for a very obvious reason. It was as well that he had already made up his mind to return the confiscated radio set, for he was not a man to be bribed into doing favours against his better judgement.

However, it would be churlish to question the thought behind the gift, Mr Wilkins decided. Much as it offended him as a work of art, he would have to hang it on the wall – for the time being, at any rate – or Bromwich's feelings would be hurt.

So he propped *Country Scene in Spring* on the mantelshelf next to the photograph of last year's cricket team, and glanced in the cupboard to make sure that the miniature radio was ready to hand. After that, he yawned his way off to bed . . . One way and another, it had been an exhausting birthday!

Chapter 12

Full Circle

Shortly after breakfast the following morning, Bromwich sauntered into the common-room, conducting an invisible orchestra with a pocket comb.

Jennings glanced up from his library book and noticed the earphone and the lead disappearing into the conductor's pocket. "So you got your radio back, then!" he observed.

"Yes, of course – thanks to me and my crafty plot." Bromwich switched off the set and removed the earphone. "I spent all day yesterday working on Old Wilkie – being nice to him because it was his birthday, and all that flannel. So when you gave me the message about seeing him after breakfast, I knew I'd done the trick."

"Who are you kidding! It was all due to me that he gave it back," Jennings protested.

Bromwich bridled indignantly. "Of course it wasn't! Who chatted him up all day to put him in a good mood? Who passed him his sandwiches on the picnic? Who sat next to him all the way home, telling him jokes? Who—?"

"You're crazy! That sort of thing doesn't cut any

ice with Old Wilkie." Jennings felt justified in claiming the credit that was due. "What really tipped the balance was me saving him hundreds of pounds by not having to smash the garage up. That was a better sort of favour than just passing him mouldy sandwiches."

"Ah, yes, but what you don't realize—"

"There's no point in arguing about it, anyway," Jennings broke in. "What matters is that you've got your set back. So now, if you don't mind, you can hand over my old master painting and then we'll be quits."

A slow smile twisted the corners of Bromwich's mouth, and he twirled the earphone on the end of its lead like a propeller.

"I can't very well do that," he confessed. "I gave it to Old Wilkie for a birthday present. It was all part of the treatment."

"You did – *what*!" Jennings was outraged. Such conduct was a shameful violation of the rights of property.

"Well, why not!" the culprit defended himself. "I wanted to give him *something*, and considering it was your fault he'd confiscated my radio, I reckoned you ought to do something to help."

"So I *did* do something to help! I put him in the right mood, saving him all those hundreds of pounds."

"Huh! That's what you think! It was my birthday present scheme that did the trick."

"Well, I like your cheek! You're a gruesome specimen, Bromo. You pinched my painting. I could have you prosecuted! I could have you arrested!"

"Go on, then – arrest me! I challenge you!"

Their voices rose as the quarrel warmed up, and a group of third-formers who were busying themselves within earshot closed in on the contestants to find out what the trouble was about. As soon as they had gleaned the facts, they started debating the matter amongst themselves.

"Of *course* old Bromo's in the wrong," Rumbelow maintained at the top of his voice. "It wasn't his to give away. He was supposed to be looking after it."

"Ah, but if it's been given to Old Wilkie as a present, it belongs to him now," Atkinson shouted back. "You can't give somebody a birthday present one day, and then ask for it back next morning."

"That's right. It's just Jennings' bad luck," Temple agreed. "I don't see that he's got much to moan about. I dare say Old Wilkie will let him go and have a look at it once a week, if he asks him properly."

"That's not the point. You don't understand about security," Venables thundered. "It's like, say, for instance, if somebody wants to borrow a thousand pounds from the bank . . ."

The argument raged on in various parts of the room, growing louder and more futile with every fresh twist in the debate.

Jennings and Bromwich had to stop quarrelling because neither could hear what the other was saying. But when at last there came a lull in which he could make himself heard, Jennings said, "Well, anyway, Bromo, I wouldn't have minded so much if it'd been just an ordinary old picture, but this one was a genuine old master. The woman at the sale told me: she said I ought to hang on to it, in case it was priceless."

Bromwich stopped twirling his earphone and perched himself on the radiator. He, too, felt calmer now that the argument had run its course.

"You don't think I'd have given it to Old Wilkie if it had been any good, do you!" he demanded. "I had my doubts all along, and just to make sure I took it to Mr Hind first, and asked him what it was worth."

The group quietened down to listen. "And what did he say?" asked Venables.

Bromwich giggled at the recollection. "He said it might come in handy for anyone who wanted a bit of canvas to patch a hole in a bell tent."

The news was greeted with a guffaw of laughter. Jennings pulled a face; then his expression cleared and he, too, started to laugh.

"Bang goes my chance of ending up a millionaire," he said with mock solemnity. "Pity about that! I was relying on my old master to make my fortune for me."

Just then, the bell rang for morning assembly. As the boys streamed out into the corridor, Rumbelow said, "Now you've got your set back, Bromo, I reckon you ought to let old Jennings borrow it some time, to make up for his picture."

"I might – when I'm not using it," Bromwich agreed. He thought for a moment and added, "Not next week, though. Not next week on *any* account."

"Why not?"

"Because England are playing the West Indies at Leeds, that's why!" Bromwich gave a hollow laugh. "Catch me lending Jennings my set when there's a Test Match on! I'm not going through all that hoo-hah of chatting up Old Wilkie all over again."

On Sunday afternoon Jennings and Darbishire paid another visit to their camp on the Downs. Admittedly, their present plans fell far short of their earlier intentions. No longer could they look forward to cooking tasty dishes, and with the tunnel stripped of its mysteries there was no point in further exploration.

Even so, it was still their own personal cave. The thrill of discovery had been theirs, and they could still look forward to the adventure of occupation.

So, once again, they made the long hot trek through the gorse jungle in the hope of snatching a brief respite from school routine in the sanctuary of their hide-out.

Unfortunately, their plans were thwarted. Upon arrival, they found that Mr Arrowsmith had been there before them, and had blocked the entrance from side to side with a spider's web of barbed wire fastened to stout chestnut posts. The farmer was taking no chances in preventing his maverick ewe from straying into danger a second time; and in making the cave sheep-proof, he had made it boy-proof, as well.

"Coo, swizzle! Mouldy old chizz. Flipping well not fair," Jennings complained. And then, as the first shock of disappointment passed away, he added, "Still, I suppose you couldn't expect anything else, really. That old sheep would have died if we hadn't found her in time."

Darbishire knelt in front of the entrance, peering in through the wire fence. "Pity about my famous cave paintings. They look ever so real from here."

Jennings grinned. "Perhaps that's why Mr Arrowsmith wired the cave up: perhaps he couldn't stand the sight of them."

"Ah, but he might have done it specially to protect them. The barbed wire will keep the vandals out, you see. So when, in the dim and distant future, this famous archaeologist bloke comes along—"

"What archaeologist bloke?"

"How do I know? He won't be born for another five thousand years. But somebody's bound to discover my paintings some day, just as they did at Lascaux. And then, of course, he'll become famous and—"

Jennings guffawed with derision. "Lucky old him! I hope they give him a medal."

"Why not! It'd be the sensation of the seventieth century. I can see it all happening!"

Darbishire rose to his feet and strode, frowning and straight-faced, to a nearby hillock. With mock pomposity he declaimed: "Ladies and Gentlemen! . . . For my lecture this evening, I propose to deal with the works of that celebrated cave artist, C.E.J. Darbishire who, as you know, lived 'way back in the Dark Ages of the twentieth century. Few people at that time recognized the genius who was living in their midst, but fortunately for posterity—"

The lecturer broke off and dodged as his companion threw a clod of earth at him.

"I'm the audience, chucking rotten eggs," Jennings explained. "Fantastically good lecture, Darbi! Wake me up when it's over."

There was nothing much to do after that, but make their way back to school for the five o'clock roll call.

"It's bad luck about the camp, of course," Jennings observed as they followed the footpath past the farm. "Still, I'm not worried. I'll soon think of something else to do on Sunday afternoons."

When the bell rang for the end of evening prep on Monday, there was the usual mad rush of third-formers to claim possession of the junior tennis court.

Jennings and Darbishire were slow off the mark, owing to time wasted in disentangling the knots in the laces of Darbishire's tennis shoes.

"I bet Temple, or some frightful oik, tied them up on purpose, so they could bag first set on the court," Darbishire complained, tugging at the knots with clumsy fingers.

"Well, you can't prove it, so don't waste time making speeches," Jennings retorted, swinging his racket in practice shots. "We can still bag second set, if we get a move on."

As expected, they found the court already occupied when they arrived at the far end of the playing-field. Venables, Temple, Atkinson and Martin-Jones were getting ready to settle the doubles championship between The Earth and Outer Space.

"You want to be a bit quicker getting your shoes on," Temple told Darbishire with a knowing smile, as he wound up the net.

Darbishire sniffed and turned away. Unable to prove his suspicions, he decided to treat the gibe with disdain.

Jennings wasn't one to hang about doing nothing.

"Come on, Darbi, we can play cricket while they're having their set. Famous Test Match – England versus West Indies. Bags I be England and bat first!"

He grabbed a tennis ball from the box beside the net-post, and with the two rackets under his arm he scampered away to the top of the bank.

"This is the wicket," he announced, taking up a stance with one of the rackets in front of the garden roller. "You can bowl as fast as you like, as it's only a tennis ball."

"Well, bags you don't slosh it as hard as you can," the bowler called back, throwing down his blazer to mark the bowling crease. He fielded the ball as Jennings tossed it down the pitch towards him. "It's almost impossible to bowl anyone out with a soft ball. Look at the size of your racket: it's twice as wide as a cricket bat."

"I know, but look at the size of the wicket: this old roller's ten times as big as a set of stumps," the batsman argued. "Anyway, if you can't get me out, I'll retire when I've made fifty."

The West Indian bowling was somewhat erratic, the first three balls pitching so wide of the wicket that the England batsman had to run sideways to meet the delivery.

"Oh, for goodness sake, Darbi! Bung down a straight one," Jennings protested.

The next ball, though straight, came gliding gently down the pitch at such an inviting trajectory that the batsman couldn't resist the temptation to smite it as hard as he could.

It was a satisfying stroke! The tennis ball soared into the air and sailed away high over the bowler's head. Losing height at last, it dropped to earth far beyond the tennis court in a patch of long grass and nettles.

Darbishire was furious. "Hey, that's not fair! You promised!"

"Sorry, I just *had* to; I couldn't resist it."

"Well, you flipping well go off and find it, then!"

"Fossilised fish-hooks, no! You're the fielding side – not me! It was your fault for bowling an easy one."

Grumbling to himself, the bowler set off at a crawling pace to go and fetch the ball. On the way, he underlined his protest by stopping at intervals to admire the view. He wasn't going to hurry!

He was gone for a long time, for when at last he reached the patch of long grass, he couldn't find the ball. He poked about vaguely with the toe of his shoe, unwilling to show any enthusiasm for the task in hand.

For a few minutes after Darbishire's departure, Jennings stood beside the roller trying to balance the makeshift bat on his forehead. Tiring of this, he looked round for some form of diversion, and saw Rumbelow standing by himself near the tennis court, tossing a ball into the air and catching it one-handed as it fell.

"Hey, Rumbo, give us a bowl!" Jennings called out, and took up his stance with the racket against the garden roller.

"OK!" Rumbelow came hurrying up the slope, swinging his arm round and round to loosen his muscles. Reaching the top, he broke into his bowling run, and was going at full speed by the time he reached the bowling crease.

"Fast one coming up!" he shouted, as the ball left his hand.

It certainly *was* a fast one! Jennings stepped forward, swinging his racket to meet it with a lively off-drive . . . It was not until the missile was hurtling up off the pitch towards him, that he saw that it wasn't a discoloured tennis ball, as he had supposed, but a hard leather cricket ball.

It was too late to check his stroke. There was a sharp crack as ball and racket made contact. As they did so, the racket split in two between handle and frame, and the ball hit the roller with a resounding clang, bounced off at an angle and rolled down the slope.

Rumbelow was jubilant. "How's that! First ball, middle stump, dead on the wicket," he crowed, flinging up his arms in triumph. "I told you to watch out for a fast one!"

Jennings stopped staring at the broken racket. "You clumsy great maniac! Look what you've done!" he stormed.

"*Me*! It wasn't my fault. You said, 'Give me a bowl,' and I—"

"I didn't know it was a *hard* ball. I thought it was a tennis ball."

Rumbelow shrugged. "Bit late to tell me that now. After all, if you invite somebody to play *cricket*, you'd hardly expect them to—"

At that point in the argument Darbishire arrived back, still grumbling, with the tennis ball he had retrieved from the long grass. At a glance, he took in what had happened, and laughed uproariously at the sight of his friend with the handle of the racket in one hand and the frame in the other.

"Jennings' famous two-piece racket!" he chortled. "Serves you right for sloshing my bowling and making me go and find it. You won't be able to use the tennis court any more, now, will you!"

Jennings gave him a look. "You can stop laughing, Darbi. It wasn't my tennis racket – it was *yours*."

"*What*!" Darbishire was incensed. "Well, of all the cheek! Who said you could—?"

"I've only just noticed it," Jennings broke in. "I just happened to be using yours – purely by chance. There's my racket, look, behind the roller."

"Just the sort of thing you *would* do," Darbishire fumed. "You're not fit to be in charge of an oil-fired

150

wellington boot, let alone somebody else's tennis racket. That's the second one of mine you've busted this term."

Jennings conceded the point. "We're back where we started then, aren't we?" he observed. "Mind you, I'm sorry and all that, but it was just as much your fault really, because—"

"*My* fault! Of *course* it wasn't my fault!" Darbishire could hardly contain his wrath. "All right then, Jennings, I've finished with you, for ever. Don't think I'm your friend any more, because I'm not. I've just about had enough!"

Mr Carter was the master on duty that evening. Strolling round the playing-field on his tour of supervision, he came across Jennings and Darbishire, red-faced and shouting, each brandishing half a tennis racket with threatening gestures. Close at hand stood Rumbelow, wearing a ghoulish smile and stirring up the hostility whenever it tended to flag.

"What's going on here?" the master demanded.

The boys broke off the quarrel in mid-insult and looked a little sheepish.

"Nothing, sir. Nothing at all, really," Jennings assured him.

"That's often the case. It usually turns out to be nothing at all when you get to the heart of the matter," Mr Carter said. "You'd better tell me, all the same."

"Well, sir, there was a bit of an accident. I've just broken Darbishire's tennis racket for the second time," Jennings explained. "Or rather, not the same racket twice over, if you follow me. I mean, two rackets once only, if you see what I mean."

Mr Carter saw what he meant – and listened to the rest of the details. Then he said, "It's unfortunate of course, but it's hardly worth coming to blows about. And it's easily put right: there's a whole stack of unclaimed tennis rackets that don't belong to anybody in the lost property cupboard. Come and see me before you go up to bed, Darbishire, and I'll find one you can have."

Darbishire's eyes sparkled behind his dusty spectacles. "What – to *keep*, sir? For my very own? Free of charge?"

"Why not! They're no use to anybody lying in the cupboard. Some of them have been there for years."

"Coo, thank you, sir. Thank you very much indeed."

"That's all right. In fact, if only you'd come and told me when the first accident happened," Mr Carter informed them, "I could have fixed both of you up with perfectly good rackets without any trouble at all."

Mr Carter resumed his stroll round the playing-field, and Rumbelow wandered away to continue his one-handed catching practice.

Left to themselves, Darbishire turned to Jennings, all troubles forgotten. "How about that, then! Take you on at singles after prep tomorrow?"

Jennings grinned. "OK, Darbi. Just you and me, eh!"

As always, the quarrel had ended as abruptly as it had broken out. Darbishire sank down on the grass and said, "Pity we didn't think of going to Mr Carter the first time, wasn't it! It would have saved us an awful lot of trouble."

"Saved us trouble! Fossilised fish-hooks, that's not the way to look at it." Jennings dismissed the idea with a snort of derision. His own views on the matter were somewhat different.

Why, if they had gone to Mr Carter the first time, he argued, there would have been no need for him to have attended the auction sale, which meant that he wouldn't have come back from the dentist's with a cooking-stove. The cooking-stove had given them the idea of setting up camp, and without the camp there would have been no cave paintings. And that meant that they wouldn't have taken Venables and Temple to see the bogus art treasures, so they wouldn't have been on hand to rescue the stranded sheep.

"And all the other things too – me losing my clothes and you losing your glasses, and everything," Jennings went on, warming to his theme. "None of these things would have happened if we'd got our rackets the easy way." He perched himself on the roller, strumming the strings of the broken racket like a banjo. "I'm really pleased we didn't go to Mr Carter. Look at all the fun we'd have missed."

His companion grinned. "Typically Jennings!" he murmured.

"What d'you mean – typically me?"

"Nothing much: I was only thinking." Darbishire scratched his nose to aid the process of thought. He had always been aware that his own easy-going attitude to life's problems was poles apart from his friend's lively determination to meet trouble halfway; but he'd never before tried to put the thought into words.

"It's just your crazy way of carrying on," he said at length. "If there's a simple answer to anything, you don't want to know about it." Darbishire sighed and shook his head. "You like doing things the hard way, don't you!"